THE JOINT BASE CHARLESTON MURDERS

The Pilot and Pianist Mystery Series

THE JOINT BASE CHARLESTON MURDERS

The Pilot and Pianist Mystery Series

M.W. Burdette

ISBN-13: 9798600360419

Original Publication Date: 2021. Published in the United States of America by Amazon.com.

For Allen Johnson

A Special Friend

CONTENTS

Prologue

Why would someone use a $268 million dollar airplane to eliminate a problem that could be rectified by a simple "hit and run" on the streets of Historic Charleston in the Battery? The very minimum crew operating the Lockheed C-5 Galaxy aircraft is from 8 to 12 people. The crew can be expanded to a number exceeding 20 people, depending on the scope of the mission and the length of the actual flight. What were the odds that one of the pilots would have commandeered the large airplane to commit suicide? Not beyond the realm of disbelief, but not a common, verifiable thing that happened in the U.S. Air Force. Before a pilot is assigned to fly missions in multi-million-dollar aircraft, the routine procedure is for them to undergo a series of psychological tests to determine the soundness of mind that is required to perform the task. Plus, there were always two pilots and many times three: a flight commander, a first pilot, and a co-pilot, flying the huge airplane, along with other engineers and technicians. Logic would dictate that if one of the pilots had a death wish, the odds were that the other two pilots could prevent the disturbed pilot from commandeering the airliner and plunging it to the ground to commit suicide. There might be exceptions to this rule, but the likelihood of suicide-by-airplane was remote, at best. And, if suicide is ruled out in cases such as the C5-A Galaxy crash, that leaves only two other possible causes for a crash—mechanical failure or sabotage. The C5-A Galaxy was put into service in 1969, and in fifty years of service—flying in and out of war-torn countries and in domestic training—only three aircraft had crashed where loss of life was encountered. Mechanical failure had not been a factor for decades with the gigantic aircraft. A few minor crash landings had done some damage to the fuselage of the huge war bird, but no significant injuries were recorded. In other words, the safety record of the C5-A Galaxy was excellent.

Now, on a routine training mission out of Charleston, South Carolina, a C5-A Galaxy had crashed and left no survivors. Something didn't fit with the official reporting of the accident. The U.S. Air Force, and the Joint Chiefs of Staff for the United States Government wanted, and needed, a more detailed investigation into why such a tragedy happened. The NTSB could determine if a bomb had been used, or some other form of sabotage employed, to bring the gigantic bird down. The Air Force was as concerned as to *why* and not just *what* happened to cause this tragedy. To discover those answers, they would need someone with both familiarization with jet aircraft operation and detective skills to delve into the case and ferrate out some answers that made sense. That was a rare combination of skills that was not easily found in the general public. Most retired Air Force pilots became commercial pilots until forced to retire at sixty years of age. Few detectives were pilots of any kind, much less pilots of supersonic jet aircraft. Needless to say, the choice of investigator for this particular case was very limited.

The commanding general of the U.S Air Force had his staff research every ex-pilot who had every flown jet aircraft and were now retired. From that list they narrowed the potential investigators down to just a few potential candidates. Of the three ex-pilots with detective skills, one was now deceased, one was in his late 70s and suffering from Alzheimer's, and the other was the police chief of a small city in the State of Alabama. The choice was not really hard to make—CPT Neal Butch Todd, USAF Retired, was their man.

Chief Butch Todd had been the chief of the Ashburn Police Department for six months, had figured out how to run the department as its lead man, *and* still carved out enough time to help his Chief of Detectives, Claire Cavendish, with the more challenging cases that came her way. Missing dogs, stray children from school, and the decapitation of parking meters on

Main Street were not the kind of crimes that required his attention. Once the determination of the murders of the professors at Ashburn University had been solved, most other crimes seemed to stand in the shadow of their past success at solving the Ashburn University murders case. Butch liked to go out into the field with Claire, rekindle the gum-shoe detective status he held before becoming the Chief of Police, and relive the days when they first became partners under the command of CPT Freddie Black, the previous chief who had abruptly moved his family to Colorado to seek medical assistance for his teenage daughter. Things had worked out as best as could be expected under the circumstances. The last phone call he ever expected to receive was from a person who rubbed elbows with the President of the United States on a weekly basis.

Chapter 1

A Call for Help

Neal Butch Todd, retired U.S. Air Force pilot and now both a detective for the City of Ashburn and the Ashburn Police Chief, was sitting at this desk, reading the local newspaper and drinking possibly the worst cup of coffee ever created by a well-meaning sergeant.

"Hey, Leon," Butch called out to the desk sergeant on duty. "Who made the coffee this morning? I truly believe it could stand up vertical without a cup!"

Leon did not answer back, but rather, PFC Elene Connally answered him. "I made it, smart ass. Complaining about the free coffee again?" They both had a laugh over the continuing saga of bad coffee at police precincts.

Butch had come to the office by himself this morning because Claire was following up with one of the stores in downtown Ashburn about a potential robbery that had occurred over the weekend. Butch sat behind his desk, sipped on his mug of coffee, and began to look at the unopened mail on his desk. In most cases, Elene was tasked to open routine mail, sort it, and deliver it to whoever was probably going to be following up on a particular incident. Today's mail was somewhat different. Fall was in the air, it was Monday morning, and two days of mail always presented something unexpected that eventually wound up on Butch's desk. Only one unopened envelope was sitting alone in front of him this morning. At first glance, it looked official. The last time Butch saw envelopes that resembled the one he was now staring at was when he was in the active U.S. Air Force. He picked it up, turned it this way and that, and decided that he had to eventually open it, so there was no time like the present. As he began to read the letter from General Tecumseh Hamilton Brown, Chief of Staff for the U.S. Air Force, he began to get a lump in his throat that prevented him from swallowing. The letter's content included the words below:

Captain Todd, Retired, we need to talk in person. The subject is highly sensitive and still classified at this time. I need for you to meet me at the Pentagon on October 10, 2019, at 11:00 AM. Please present yourself, and your counsel if you want to be represented, to the entrance of the Pentagon no later than 7:30 AM on October 10th. You will be escorted to an office in the Pentagon for a secure meeting. Other than your personal representative, you are not to discuss this meeting. If you have issues getting off work to come to meet me, please call my office at 555-423-2323 and someone will speak to your supervisor. This is not a request, but rather an order. See you then.

The letter was signed, General Tecumseh Hamilton Brown, U.S.A.F., Chief of Staff. At first, Butch looked at the letter trying to think who of his remaining friends in the Air Force could pull off a caper such as this. It looked so official. He worried for a moment, then he did the only logical thing that he knew to do. He called the Pentagon.

"This is the Pentagon. How may I direct your call?" a pleasant voice said over the phone line.

"My name is CPT Neal Butch Todd, Retired, and I wanted to speak to someone in General Tecumseh Brown's office. Can you help connect me?"

"I'll put you through to the general's desk sergeant. Hopefully, he will be able to help you." She transferred the call and Butch could hear the subsequent ringing on the line.

"General Brown's Office. May I help you?"

"Yes, please. My name is CPT Neal Butch Todd, and…" before Butch could continue, he was connected with another number. When the voice on the other line answered, there was no doubt that he was talking to *the man*.

"General Brown here. To whom am I speaking?" Suddenly, having heard this authoritarian voice, Butch had lost his own voice, or at least the memory of what he was going to say. "Are you still there?" the voice seemed angry now. "Speak up, or I'll hang up!"

"Yes, Sir. Sorry I went blank on you for a moment. My name is CPT Neal Butch Todd, Retired, and I think someone may be playing a joke on me. I hate to have you confirm it, but I received a somewhat official looking letter that requested that I meet you next week at the Pentagon. I just wanted to verify that it was fake."

"Why do you think it's fake, Captain? Do you think I have time to waste trying to imitate a national emergency? It is real, and I need for you to be at the Pentagon at precisely the date and time the letter requested. Will you need assistance on my part to be excused from your current employer?" Butch's head was spinning like a top. This was real!

"Well, Sir, it might make it easier if someone from your office contacted the mayor of my town and request my presence. His name is Sam Hannity," and Butch repeated the mailing address and the private telephone number to the general.

"Consider it done, Captain."

"Begging your pardon, Sir, but I'm no longer a Captain in the U.S. Air Force. I'm the Chief of Police in Ashburn, Alabama."

"The hell you say! You're CPT Todd if I say you are! When you meet me in Virginia next week, I'll have your reactivation orders. You have been assigned to a very serious task that will be performed under cover and in secret. More will be explained to you when you arrive. You may bring an assistant, if you so prefer, or else I'll assign you an assistant once you're here. Since this is not a secure line, Captain, that's all I will say about it. Someone will contact your Mayor Hannity and square things with him. Any questions?"

"No, Sir," Butch replied, suddenly thrust back into non-voluntary compliance from which he had escaped just a couple of years ago. Butch heard the line go dead and the dial tone reappear. The phone call that would change his immediate future was in the books!

* * *

Butch hung up the telephone and tried to recall what had just happened. It was like a dream—no, a nightmare. He had left the military service because he no longer wanted someone telling him what to do, how to do it, and when to do it. That story was in his past. Now, he gets a letter out of nowhere telling him that he's been re-inducted for some top-secret reason. Something was wrong here, and he would find out before he hauled his ass 719 miles to the Pentagon in Virginia. He noticed that Claire had returned to the office after her early encounter with the businessman in town.

"You're deep in thought," she said. "What's got your mind boggled this early in the day?"

"I'm going to tell you, but you're not going to believe it. Come into my office and close the door behind you." Claire did as she was asked without needing anymore persuasion. She had seen Butch in serious moods, romantic moods, and silly moods. This was one of his more serious ones.

"I'm all ears," Claire said. "Something seems to have made you uneasy, and I can only remember one or two times since I've known you that you were spooked about things. Care to share?"

"I will tell you, but you will have to promise that you will share this information with no one else."

"You're beginning to scare me, Butch."

"I received an "eyes only" letter from the U.S. Air Force today." He opened the letter, spun it around so she could read it, and waited for the subject matter to register with her. She raised her eyebrows, looked back at Butch, and pushed the letter back to him.

"What does it mean? Maybe it's one of your old military buddies trying to pull a trick over on you. What are the odds this letter is genuine?"

"One-hundred percent, as of a few minutes ago."

"You're going to have to explain that answer to me, because it makes no sense. How could you possibly know it is genuine? Did you call the Pentagon?" She laughed when she asked the question, but she stopped laughing when it occurred to her that Butch was not laughing with her.

"In short, I *did* call the Pentagon, and I spoke to the general myself. He was not amused that I found his note to me as laughable or possibly a joke."

"Oh," is all Claire said in response.

"Yeah. Oh." Butch looked despondent as he continued to explain the nature of the telephone call with General Brown.

"Wait a minute. You're retired. Correct?"

"I am."

"Then how can you be forced to follow orders from the general of the U.S.A.F.? Doesn't make sense to me."

"Let's see if I can help you understand. When a person takes a commission to protect the United States of America in any branch of the military service, they are subject to recall by their branch of service indefinitely—even after retirement. It's in the oath of allegiance."

"No way!"

"Actually, it's true. There are some exceptions to being reinstated, but it is generally accepted that if Uncle Sam wants you back, you have to go—at least for a limited period."

"That's crazy. Did you know that when you agreed to become an officer?"

"You are told those types of things, but you never think you will be one of the few retired officers recalled to duty. And a young man of 20 years of age never thinks about such consequences."

"So, they want you back as a jet pilot?"

"To be honest with you, Claire, I'm not sure why they want me back. That's what we will find out when we visit the Pentagon on the 10th of October."

"We? You said, 'We.' Don't you mean, 'You?'"

"No. I meant *we*."

"Well, I've got to admit that you've stumped me with that revelation. How in the world am I qualified to help you, assuming that the mayor would permit my absence, and that I would agree to go to Charleston, South Carolina, on this field trip?"

"First of all, you work for me, and not the mayor. If I decide that I need you on my task force to help the U.S. Air Force and the U.S. Government, I doubt the mayor would complain too loudly. Second, this is not a field trip, as you suggest. Whatever it is, and I don't know exactly what that might be at this time, is important enough for the U.S. Air Force to call me back to active duty, and for the Joint Chief of Staff to the President to personally speak to us about it. And, last but not least, you are the only person I trust to have my back no matter what happens!"

"Assuming all of that is true, how do you think the mayor can get by with his chief of police and primary detective working out of the office for a few days or weeks? Have you thought of that?"

"Actually, I have. I'm not sure what we will be doing, nor how long that tour of duty might be, but it's important enough that I think I can coach the mayor on getting help from the general while we're gone to cover our jobs."

"Now, you have really lost me. Please explain."

"Let's assume that they will need us for two weeks for whatever tasks this top-secret duty demands. We will suggest that the general send a minimum of two U.S. Air Force Security Forces people to cover for us while we are actively helping him with whatever his task winds up being. They come to Ashburn—we go to the Pentagon. It's that simple. They are probably better at security than our own officers are, and they are disciplined and will do as they are told without questioning a command. They want two of us for temporary duty; we get two of theirs as long as you and I are away. Simple math."

"Who would be in charge of the precinct, the current officers, and these two new security force people while you are away?"

“I’m thinking PFC Elene Connally.”

“Not SGT Leon Cumberland? He outranks her.”

“That’s true, but we can make Elene Acting Police Chief while we are gone. When we return, everything returns to normal.”

“You know what happened the last time that was done in Ashburn. Are you not superstitious that something might happen to you, and you wind up in a similar situation as Freddie Black?”

“I’m not superstitious, Claire. I can’t think of another way to make all this happen on such short notice. Have you got a better idea?” Claire sat quietly for a moment, looked up at Butch wordlessly, and nodded no.

“OK. Then we do it my way.”

“We don’t even know what they are going to ask you to do. Have you thought about that?”

“I have. I suspect it will have something to do with jet aircraft and detective work—some combination of those things.”

“I guess we won’t know until we make the trip to the Pentagon. Right?”

“Correct. That’s pretty much the situation. Now, let’s go see Mayor Hannity and see if the general has spoken to him about all of this.” Claire got up from her desk, grabbed her purse, and they headed out to see the mayor.

“Let’s walk, Butch. It’s such a pleasant fall day. Maybe the good weather, great company, and brief exercise will clear our heads and help us make a good decision when we’re offered some choices by the mayor.” She smiled at him and they began a brisk walk toward city hall. They got to the reception area and asked it Mayor Hannity was in the office.

"Yes, Chief, he is in, but as you know, he normally works by appointment."

"Believe me when I tell you that he will want to speak to us as soon as possible. Will you please call back and see if he can work us into his early morning schedule? We are willing to wait in the lobby until he can get to us. It's an emergency."

The secretary, who also acted as a gatekeeper for the mayor, called by and told the mayor that he had two visitors who needed to see him immediately, assuming he was available. She told him that the two visitors were the Chief of Police and Chief of Detectives. Almost immediately, Mayor Hannity appeared in the lobby and walked immediately to his police officers.

"What's up, Butch?" the mayor asked. "I understand you need to speak to me about something of vital interest to you. May I ask what that might be?" Butch whispered something in the mayor's ear, and he agreed to carry on the conversation in his office, rather than in the precinct outer lobby. Claire and Butch followed the mayor down the hall to his office, took a chair in front of the mayor's large, leather desk, and waited for the mayor to take his chair behind his desk. Once he had made himself comfortable, he began the conversation again.

"OK, we are now in my secure office. What is so important that we needed to go through that ceremony in the lobby?" Butch and Claire thought the mayor was somewhat sarcastic when questioning them, but they let it slide.

"Mayor, have you been contacted by a General Tecumseh Brown of the U.S. Air Force?"

"Tecumseh Brown? That sounds like someone from the Civil War, Butch. What's this all about? You have my total attention."

"I really don't know where to start, Mayor, so I'll just start at the beginning."

"That would be a good plan," he answered and smiled warmly at his chief of police.

"This morning when I arrived at work, there was an envelope waiting for me that looked very official from the U.S. Air Force. After opening it and reading the message from the U.S. Air Force Commanding General, the person I just spoke of, I first thought it was a joke or a trick being played on me by one of my old Air Force buddies, so I thought I'd prove it to myself by contacting General Brown's office directly. From when I first placed the call to his office, until he hung up the phone after giving me specific instructions about what he wanted me to do, only ten minutes had transpired. What he said was that I was being reinstated as an Air Force officer, and that I would need to meet him on October 10th, that's next week, at the Pentagon. He instructed me to bring an assistant with me, and he swore me to silence. He said he would be contacting you today to speak to you about the situation. Are you sure you haven't received a telephone call from the Pentagon this morning?" The mayor looked worried, and he pickup up his telephone handset and asked his secretary to come into his office.

Sally Lancaster, the mayor secretary the entire time he had been in office, came into the room with a steno pad and a ballpoint pen in her hand. She was tall, slim, and a handsome woman of about fifty years of age. Butch had overheard in the past that she became an employee of the mayor's office when she was twenty-one years old, just out of Ashburn University. She had just celebrated her thirty-year anniversary as a city employee, and she was beloved by all who knew her.

"Sally, did we hear from the Pentagon this morning?"

"It's funny that you should ask, Mayor. I just took a message off the recorder from a General Brown's office. The person calling did not appear to be the general, but rather one of his associates. I'm sorry I didn't mention it to you, but the message was for you to not return the call, but rather be available at 11:00 AM for the general's call." Sally looked a little embarrassed, but there was no way she could have shared the message with Mayor Hannity until now.

"That's not a problem, Sally. Did the caller mention what the subject of the telephone call would be?"

"No, Sir. The complete message was that the call would be returned at 11:00."

"Thank you, Sally. You may go back to your desk." She nodded, turned elegantly, and walked back to her office.

"Well, that was weird," the mayor said. "I guess we will all discover what the Commanding General of the Air Force has on his mind when he calls back in thirty minutes." The mayor looked at the wall clock in his office and it registered 10:30 AM. "Butch, why don't you two get a cup of coffee and we'll wait for the call?"

"Mayor, I will get a cup of coffee, but we need to speak briefly before the general calls back at 11:00 AM," Butch said. "I have an inkling of what he may be going to request of you, and us, and I think we should be prepared to make a counteroffer." The mayor seemed to accept Butch's premise without argument. Hannity suggested they all get coffee and reassemble in his office in five minutes.

Chapter 2

Strategy

Butch Todd had learned a valuable lesson on his first air combat mission in Afghanistan. He had graduated first in his class at the Air Combat School at the Joint Base Langley-Eustis, Virginia, and he was hyped and ready to go to war against whatever foe the United States sent him. There was no question in anyone's mind that the U.S. Navy, U.S. Marines, and the U.S. Air Force had the best equipment and training in the world when it came to combat missions. What the young pilot, LT Butch Todd, learned quickly in the air over Kabul was that there was no wiggle room for do overs. If a pilot, flying a multi-million-dollar fighter jet at Mach 2.0, doesn't have a plan when he engages the enemy, there's a 50/50 chance that he won't be going home to the base after the dogfight. In the military the term for planning how to approach the enemy to ensure success is often referred to as having a strategy. In other words, if the enemy does *this*, you respond by doing *that*. The response has to be automatic, a reflex, a calculated move designed to answer the enemy's original move. Anything less and the odds of succeeding in such a dogfight are reduced greatly, and that pilot has to rely upon his luck to get him home. That's not acceptable when lives and multi-million-dollar jets are on the line. So, it was logical to Butch to have a strategy ready if, and when, the general called Mayor Hannity to ask for the chief of police's help for whatever reason he might be needing it. It was logical.

"OK, Butch. Tell me what you think is going on with the Commanding General of the U.S.A.F., and why we should have a plan to counter some request he might make. I mean, what can he do? Ask you to plan to return to active duty? Just say no."

"It's not quite that easy a fix, Sir," Butch replied. "When one joins any military branch, each commissioned officer is actually working for the President of the United States. That's why you often hear that the President is the Commander in Chief—he is the ultimate authority. When accepting that commission that officer also signs a document that states that even after retirement from that branch of service, or if that officer is encouraged to leave the service for reasons not in his or her own best interest, that officer can be called back up to serve at the pleasure of the Commander in Chief or his senior officers. So, if the U.S.A.F. wants me back for a period of time for some specific reason, I have no choice but to report. Does that help you understand the complexity of the issue?" The mayor was looking at Butch, but he was seeing someone entirely different from the employee he had come to know these past few months.

"Let's suppose I agree with you that we should have a plan going forward. How do you think that would work for us, and how will I need to sell it to General Brown?"

"The general is probably going to tell you that he wants me to come to the Pentagon for some investigative reason. Other than my recently acquired investigative skills, he could get one of many pilots to do his bidding—some who are probably still in active status. No, it has to be some combination of my current status, and my past U.S. Air Force experience that has brought him to his conclusion. I can't figure it any other way."

"Did he tell you why he wanted to speak to you when you spoke to him on the telephone? I can't imagine that he would expect you to drop everything that you are doing now and show up at the Pentagon without knowledge of why you are being summoned."

"Did you ever serve on active duty in the military, Mayor?"

"No. By the time I got to the age to serve it was an all-volunteer U.S. Army, and none of the branches of the U.S. Military was subject to the draft. I went on to graduate school, teaching, and now serving in the civilian branch of government."

"Well, I didn't ask you that to accuse you of not performing your honorable duty to our country, but rather to verify that you have never been in a situation where logic was not necessarily the driving force for making decisions. General Brown feels no need to consider our concerns to make his command decisions. Trust me on this, Mayor. We should be prepared." Although the mayor seemed to have been somewhat pacified by Butch's comments, he asked Butch to outline what he thought might be a logical scenario that the general might suggest.

"Well, I'm not sure you remember the crash of a C5-A Galaxy aircraft a few weeks back. The NTSB was called into the investigation, as usual procedure, and then nothing else was reported about the incident. We don't know how many people perished in the crash, or why the giant aircraft came crashing down to earth. Having been a pilot of a jet aircraft in the past, I Googled pertinent words that should have revealed follow up articles by various news agencies, but nothing has appeared in print, electronic or otherwise, describing what happened."

"Isn't that pretty much par for the course with the U.S. Government—need to know, and all that bullshit?"

"I agree there must be secret reports about the crash that have not made the new cycle, but for there to be nothing at all mentioned several weeks after a $250+ million-dollar airplane crashes is problematic for me. How many people died?

Shouldn't that be public knowledge since the public is paying for the plane and training?"

"I see your point. And you think General Brown may be thinking you, as a recently retired jet pilot, and now a police detective, might be able to get to the bottom of things? I have to admit, Butch, it sounds a little out there."

"Well, whatever he asks me to do will probably have to remain classified, so don't expect him to tell you very much about what he will be wanting me to do, or for how long he wants me to do it."

"You said you had a plan in mind when we speak to him. Can you elaborate on it, or is that classified, too?"

"I do, but I need for you to hear me out completely before you react to what I'm going to suggest. Will you promise me that you'll do that?"

"Sure. Spill it. What do you propose?"

"The general told me that I would need to bring an assistant with me, and I have asked Claire if she would be willing to go with me and fill that position." Before the mayor could react negatively, Butch held up both hands as if he were surrendering to an armed robber. "Please, Mayor. Just hear me out. I think you'll like what I have to say." Butch could see that the mayor was losing what little patience that he might have had when this conversation began, so he thought he should cut to the chase.

"I'm listening, Butch." The mayor looked at Claire and scrutinized her expression as Butch was explaining his plan.

"The way I see it, Mayor, is that you are in the driver's seat. You represent civilian authority, and the general represents all authority. Correct?"

"Yeah. So what? He can pull rank, can't he?"

"Maybe, but maybe not. To get to the rank of general in the military service, you have to learn how to dodge some landmines along the way. He holds the highest rank a military person can possess. The only person who outranks him is a civilian—the President." Butch was beginning to smile, and the mayor began hanging on every word.

"So, you think he can be persuaded to do what? Not take you back into the U.S. Air Force?"

"I didn't say that Mayor. However, the Commanding General of the U.S. Air Force has assets at his disposal you cannot even imagine as a civilian. He controls personnel, equipment, and gives orders that send multi-million-dollar jets into battle on a daily basis. He is not without influence. If he wants something to happen, he can usually determine a way to make it happen. Therefore, we rely on his discretion and ability to get things done so he can get his specific requests from you and me quicker. In other words, *quid pro quo*—it the oldest bartering tactic ever used on the battlefield."

"Is that legal?"

"Do you want to ask?" Butch smiled when he answered the mayor's last question.

"OK. Fill me in on your complete plan. You know, this may be just speculation, and the general may not want anything but for you to suit back up and fly some jets."

"I doubt it, Mayor. As I said, he has pilots ten years younger than me, with fresher training, younger ears, eyes, and senses—mine have be honed by war, but I also am limited by nine years of pulling Gs on my body at 1800 MPH! I know from which I speak."

"I'm assuming you will want to take Claire with you?" The mayor looked at Claire as if she were complicit in getting involved with Butch. She gave the mayor a disarming smile in return.

"I suggest you tell the general that the only way you can help him is for him to send two of his military police personnel to the Ashburn Police Department to cover for me and Claire until we return from whatever mission he has planned for us. The general can make that happen without calling *anyone*. He can simply use *National Security* as a reason for his actions. The only person who might question him is the President, or the Secretary of Defense—it won't come to that. The military police personnel should be plain clothed so as not to stir up questions that no one wants to answer. Second, you should request that he pay their salaries, as well as our expenses, as long as the special situation is in place. I can promise you that seasoned military police personnel will be totally accountable to you, assuming the general tells them that that is their job. I would also request that the general send you those airmen who hold a rank of nothing less than a tech-sergeant—that's equivalent to a staff sergeant in the U.S. Army, or an E-6. No one becomes an E-6 in any branch of the military without reenlisting and serving in foreign tours, usually in Afghanistan or Syria. They will be equipped to handle anything that may happen in Ashburn while we are away."

"Is that all?" Mayor Hannity asked with a chuckle. "Should we ask him to send us some killer drones just in case the natives get restless?" Hannity smirked, revealing to Butch and Claire that he was being facetious. They all looked the wall clock and noticed that it was almost 11:00 AM—the time for the general to call. "Anything else I need to do?"

"Be nice, Mayor. My mother always told me that honey draw bees much better than vinegar." Hannity nodded and sat motionless at his desk in anticipation for his phone to ring. At precisely 11:00 AM, the phone rang, Hannity picked up the receiver and was told to hold for General Brown.

"This is Mayor Sam Hannity, General. I have you on speakerphone, but the only people in my office are the two people you are calling in reference to. How may I help you?"

"May I call you Sam?" the general asked warmly.

"Certainly. Butch Todd, my Chief of Police and his Chief of Detectives, Ms. Claire Cavendish, are here and I want them to be able to hear both sides of this call. Do you have a problem with that?" There was a short pause, then General Brown agreed that is was appropriate for the two people who would be most affected by his phone call be included in the discussion.

"CPT Todd?" the general called out over the line.

"I'm here, General."

"Tell me more about your assistant whom you obviously have decided on as your second in command for this mission."

"Begging the General's pardon, Sir, but I'll tell you myself," Claire's cool, firm voice echoed back to him through the mayor's office. "My name is Claire Cavendish, I'm the Chief of Detectives for the Ashburn Police Department, and I am qualified and a marksman in the use of multiple weapons. I am single and I make my own decisions as to who I work with and how I accomplish that task. I have great respect for CPT Butch Todd, now the Chief of Police and my boss here in Ashburn, Alabama. My age is not important, but I can reassure you that I can handle anything you, or the U.S. Air Force throws my way. Although we don't know what you want Butch or me to do, we are a capable team, and we usually get the job done. If you need to ask me anything else, please feel free to do that now." She stopped talking, threw a grin at both the mayor and Butch, and settled back down in her chair and began to sip on her coffee. There were what seemed like minutes of silence between when Claire stopped speaking and the general started again, but it was more likely seconds and not minutes.

"Well, Ms. Cavendish, I think you'll do just fine."

"It's Detective, General. Just refer to me as detective." She winked at the two men staring at her in disbelief once more from across the room.

"Good idea, Detective," the general said, and he continued with his definition of the task he had in mind for Butch and Claire. He told them that he wanted them to look into the crash of the C5-A Galaxy in the Charleston area a few weeks ago. He wanted them to be invisible and totally independent of the NTSB, the U.S.A.F. Security Forces, and even to keep their investigation separate from the FBI and all other government security agencies. They would report directly to the general. Their work would be classified as Top Secret/Eyes Only, and they would be subject to military discipline if they leaked any information from their findings without the specific, written approval of the general himself. Did they believe that could complete such a mission, and would they be accommodating to opening such an investigation for him. He would see that they had everything that they needed to complete the job, reasonable expenses paid for their lodging, travel, and food, and unfettered access to the wreckage of the C5-A air ship, and the personnel records of everyone on board who had perished in the crash.

"There's one other thing that we need to discuss, General," Butch motioned to the mayor to enter the conversation with the requests that he and Butch had discussed an hour or so earlier.

"What is it, Mayor? Do you have a specific request?"

"Yes, I do, General," and Sam Hannity made his request for assistance from General Brown without stuttering or hesitating at all. Butch had advised the mayor to make his request, ask the closing question, and then shut up. The first person who spoke would lose the confrontation. So, that's exactly what Hannity did. There wasn't a sound in the room for over two minutes measured by the clock on the wall. Then the general spoke.

"Mayor, I will agree to everything you ask for, but with the understanding that when CPT Todd and Detective Cavendish leave your office that you don't expect or even ask for an update from them about their mission for me and the U.S. Air Force. Is that a deal?"

"In other words, General, this conversation didn't ever happen?"

"Something like that. Do you agree?"

"Yes, Sir. I will reluctantly lend you my Chief of Police and Chief of Detectives until they have performed whatever task you need from them. Once that is done, I expect you to release them both back to my custody and their civilian status. And, as far as I'm concerned, this conversation never existed and the investigation you have planned for them didn't either. Agreed?"

"Agreed, Mayor. I need the captain and your detective ASAP. You can expect my people in your office tomorrow morning at 08:00 hours. Good day." After his salutation, he was gone.

The mayor looked at Butch and Claire and nodded his head with satisfaction. He was getting help to cover for the loss of two very important people in his department, and he would have to live with the fact that he could have lost Butch indefinitely had his Chief of Police not been so savvy.

"Damned good thing we had that little discussion, Butch. Tell me the truth. How did you know what he was going to ask for?"

"Just chalk it up to me being married to the U.S.A.F. for nine years, Mayor. You just learn a few things when you're married that you'll never forget." They all laughed and Butch and Claire said their goodbyes and left the mayor's office.

"Pretty damned smart move, Butch. I think we should celebrate with a roll in the hay after work," she said, smiling and winking at him at the same time.

"Oh, you haven't heard the best part." Claire looked at Butch with suspicion.

"Really? What did I miss?"

"I'll fill you in once we land in Virginia at the Pentagon."

Chapter 3

The Pentagon

Butch contacted General Brown's office and suggested that they come to the Pentagon quietly, and not in such a way so their trip could be discovered or monitored by any other government agency. Butch suggested that they catch a flight to Virginia through the general's connections at the U.S.A.F., 117th Wing Group, commanded by MAJ Bennington. Since training flights could be planned by the local air command group, submitted to the general's executive officer for final approval, and passed directly to the general's desk, they could fly directly into Joint Base Anacostia—Bolling AFB—drive, and be escorted by a staff car directly to the general's office at the Pentagon—no one would be the wiser. The general thought it was a brilliant idea, and they were set to leave from Birmingham the next morning on a Gulfstream, G700, military jet that would get them to Bolling AFB in style. The G700 was configured to carry from five to twelve passengers comfortably, had a full galley available for fine dining, and flew just below the speed of sound—Mach .90. They could leave Birmingham at 8:00 AM local time, and arrive at Bolling AFB at 8:30 local time, due to gaining an hour of time with the time zone change. Figuring less than an hour to get to the Pentagon from three miles away, they should be able to meet the general at 11:00 AM with time to spare.

On October 11th, they arrived at the 117th Air Wing at 7:30 AM, checked in with the flight desk, were seated on the luxurious G700, and offered coffee, soft drinks, orange juice, or water to drink. They both opted for coffee. Claire had flown on jumbo jets to Europe when she was touring, or on commuter planes in the U.S. when she was traveling only a few hundred miles for a concert. She had never seen the inside of a Gulfstream airplane, much less flown in one. She hated to act ignorant of certain facts, but she simply had to ask Butch some basic questions about this beautiful aircraft.

"I am assuming this jet cost a lot of money to purchase. Would I be correct in assuming it cost more than $20 million?" Butch barely looked up when he answered her question.

"This is the G700—Gulfstream's largest and newest entry into the business world to fly important people anywhere in the world, and many times on one tank of fuel. The baby brother of this bird, the G550, which entered the market in 2016, was priced at $61 million. This baby is closer to $75 million."

"You have to be kidding me? Who could afford such a costly airplane, with the exception of the U.S. Military Services?"

"Don't be naïve, Claire. Think about your question. How much money do you think Apple makes a year? Or, how about Microsoft, Facebook, or Twitter? I can give you a hint. Each of those companies make enough to purchase a $75 million aircraft in less than a month. Apple had profits of $25 to $30 billion last year. And, since we're speaking of gaudy rich people, do you think the Arab oil companies fly around on chartered, worn out jets that have been handed down to them from their air force? Hardly. Every sheik in the middle east, not to mention the Russian oligarchs, either already have a G700 or they have one on order. Gulfstream will sell hundreds, if not thousands of these birds, in the next few years. There's an Arab prince who owns an A300 Airbus that cost him over $500 million, and he is not alone in such purchases. You just haven't had the opportunity to rub elbows with some of these wealthy people. They're not my favorite group of people to associate with, but they live in the shadows of societies and gobble up resources like a camel drinks water." The jet began to taxi, the pilot had illuminated the "fasten your seatbelt" light, and the elegant bird zoomed down the runway and left the ground without a sound or noticeable bump when the wheels were extracted and folded into the fuselage.

"Now that was sweet," Claire cooed. "Wow! $75 million? How did you pull this off, Butch? I'm sure this is costing the general a bunch of money to fly only us over a thousand miles to a remote U.S. Air Force base."

"If my math is correct, I imagine this trip will cost the general about $8,000 an hour for our trip. So, one and one-half hours of flight time, multiplied by $8,000, would equal about $12,000 each way."

"Damn, Butch. I feel guilty having the public pay for such luxury for our benefit."

"Why? They do it all the time for people on routine missions, not a mission like ours where the integrity of the U.S. Air Force and the commanding general might be questioned. Consider it a cost of doing business—I'm sure he has done just that."

"You know, Butch, you are constantly surprising me. I don't know whether to admire you or suspect you of something unbecoming."

"Unbecoming? Unbecoming what?" They both laughed and tilted their leather chairs back into a more comfortable position.

"You know something I just remembered?"

"What?"

"The pilot never told us we couldn't smoke on this flight. That's odd, don't you think?"

"No. The only reason people stopped smoking on airlines had very little to do with safety, but more to do with political correctness. If one person is offended, then it's not politically correct to permit such behavior. I'll bet you those stuffy, old generals smoke Havana Cuban cigars on these birds all the time." She nodded, but still seemed in awe of everything around her.

Claire and Butch dozed off on the flight and both awoke when the captain's voice came over the cabin speakers announcing their initial approach into the Washington, D.C., area. Joint Base Anacostia-Bolling was a 905-acre military installation, located in Southwest, Washington, D.C., established on 1 October 2010 during one of the government's base realignments. The Pentagon was located seven miles from the air base, an eleven-minute ride by automobile. However, both detectives were pleasantly surprised when they were met by a staff car sent by General Brown to take them to their next mode of transportation that would deposit them on the grounds of the Pentagon and let them avoid the red tape surrounding entrance into one of the most secure places in the world. The staff car pulled up alongside a magnificent sight for an aviator to behold. A Sikorsky VH-92A helicopter with camouflage paint, and absent of any discernable markings, had its rotors turning slowly anticipating its guests. They would fly onto the Pentagon grounds on an exact replica of Marine One, a $17.7 million dollar bird selected to carry the President and his cabinet to and from Camp David when the most powerful man in the free world wanted to have a little getaway from Foggy Bottom and its relentless pressure of day-to-day meetings and decisions. They climbed the steps to the main cabin and were escorted by a plain clothed Secret Service officer to their seats. Immediately upon sitting down, a pretty cabin hostess, wearing a crisp U.S.A.F. dress uniform asked them if they would like a beverage or snack on their journey to the Pentagon. What Butch and Claire wanted to order was a strong shot of bourbon or vodka, but they just shook their heads no. She went to the rear of the helicopter, strapped herself into a seat, and called the captain on the two-way radio system, indicating that the passengers were secure, and he could begin the flight to 1400 Defense Pentagon, the only address needed to locate the largest office building in the world.

According to Wikipedia, the Pentagon was constructed with up to about 6,500,000 square feet of space, and in which more than 23,000 military and civilian employees, and another 3,000 non-defense support personnel, work in each day. It has five sides, five floors above ground, two basement levels, and five ring corridors per floor with a total of 17.5 miles of corridors. When the terrorists attacked the Pentagon and flew a Boeing 757 completely loaded with passengers and fuel into the building, the unusual size and construction of the building prevented more deaths than might otherwise have occurred. To get the size of such a place into ones thought patterns, one might compare the number of people employed there to a city the size of Aberdeen, South Dakota. Assignment to the Pentagon as an active military officer usually meant that one had achieved a minimum the rank of 0-6, a Colonel in the U.S. Air Force, Army, or Marines, or a Captain in the U.S. Navy. These were considered "Junior Officers" at the Pentagon where hundreds of Generals and Admirals were also employed. Butch had a difficult time getting his mind around the fact that a full-bird colonel was fetching coffee for a Major General on a daily basis. However, having held a position at the Pentagon was a necessary achievement for anyone in the military who desired to move into the highest ranks of the services, or who wanted to compete for the Presidency one day in the future. The flight was smooth and steady, and in a matter of minutes the pilot was announcing that they were landing on the helipad at the Pentagon. He stressed to his passengers the importance of following the orders given to them about decorum and discipline, and to expect to be ushered to their final destination by armed Pentagon Force Protection Agency officers who worked directly for the Department of Defense.

The helicopter touched down, the cabin hostess unlocked the cabin door, pushed it open, and revealed a portable set of stairs that he been wheeled up to the massive helicopter to assist Butch and Claire's departure. The made their way to the bottom of the stairs and were met by a uniformed police officer who wore a sidearm and was accompanied by two other uniformed soldiers carrying M4 Carbines in the ready position. They said nothing to Claire or Butch but followed the commands of the uniformed police officer who was definitely in command of the situation. He motioned for them to get into a large black SUV, and then he and his men got into the same vehicle in seats behind Claire and Butch. The driver sped off across the tarmac and in minutes they had entered a ramp that delivered them two stories below the main Pentagon building. When they stopped, they were instructed to get out of the SUV, a wand was run over their bodies to make sure they were not armed with any weapons. No weapons of any kind were allowed in the Pentagon, with the exception of the Pentagon Force Protection Agency, and they wore sidearms that had been secured and hidden under their suit coats. There were supposedly 85 digital surveillance cameras in use in or near the Pentagon, and a small detachment of U.S. Marines on constant alert ready to defend the Pentagon and its employees at the drop of a hat.

"I think I feel about as secure as I ever will," Claire whispered to Butch as they exited the SUV and entered an elevator which would take them to the fifth floor of the West Wing of the Pentagon—to General Tecumseh Brown's office.

The elevator door opened, and two uniformed U.S. Marines stood at attention and blocked their police escort, Butch, and Claire's way to the general's office. They informed the detectives that this was a high security floor, and they would have to be searched and scanned with a handheld wand before they could proceed. Butch was beginning to get upset before the saw that the police escort was having to suffer the same treatment. He looked at Butch and Claire after they left the guards and offered a word of explanation.

"I know what you are probably thinking. We were searched with a wand before we boarded the elevator, the elevator made no stops along the way, and now we have to go through the same procedure again when the elevator opened on the fifth floor."

"Yeah, that's pretty much what I was thinking," Butch responded. "How could we have secured a weapon on a moving elevator in the most secure building in the world?"

"Magic?" Claire said with a smile on her face.

"Look, people. I don't make the rules here. To give you an example of the security checks in this building, I have been subjected to two strip searches, and four encounters with a wand already today, and it's not even 10:00 AM. That's just the way things are. One never knows who might be present on the fifth floor of this building."

"Like Vladimir or Kim Jong-un?" Mike asked, knowing his question was frivolous.

"Yes, and leaders with more clout than those two terrorists!"

"Well, the only person with more clout that Vladimir would be the President of the United States. Right?" Clair asked.

"He's here more often than you might think. Just suffice it to know that you are probably safer in this building than in the defensive underground bunker inside Cheyenne Mountain in Colorado Springs! That is, unless a 30-ton nuclear bomb is dropped on the Pentagon." He smiled and Butch and Claire began to appreciate all the care given to security.

"I'm impressed," Butch said. "Do the generals go through this protocol when they come to work each day?"

"Everyone who enters the fifth-floor west wing goes through these procedures every time they come and go from this space—except the President and the Vice-President!"

"Good to know that at least two people are considered fail-safe!" Claire said.

The captain stopped in front of a closed door, rapped twice, and a small panel opened in the door so whoever was behind the door could identify those attempting entry into the secure office. After the captain identified his two visitors, the small window closed, and the door locks clicked into the open position. The door was opened by a colonel in his OCP uniform, Official Camouflage Pattern, with no sidearm showing on his hip. The creases in his pants and shirt were impressively starched and pressed, his haircut was military style, and the only indication that he was an O-6 ranking officer was the black eagles embroidered on the shoulders of the uniform. An O-6 in the U.S Air Force, U.S. Army, and U.S. Marines was considered a full-bird colonel—only one promotion lower than a Brigadier General. In the U.S. Navy and U.S. Coast Guard, a Captain held the rank of O-6. What was impressive to Butch, who had risen only to the rank of

Captain in the U.S. Air Force, was that the lowest rank of military personnel he had seen since they had arrived at the Pentagon was an O-6. Colonels really were getting coffee for generals and admirals, as well as running their errands. He had heard this rumor for years but only now believed it to be true.

"Captain, you may release the visitors into my care. When they have completed their visit with the general, I will summon you to walk them back out." The captain acknowledged the colonel with a nod of his head, and then he was gone.

"Welcome to the Pentagon and General Tecumseh Brown's office. My name is Colonel Wright Summers, and I am the custodian of the general's office and daily affairs. I am assuming you are Captain Butch Todd and Detective Claire Cavendish. Correct?"

"That is correct, Colonel, with the exception that I am actually "retired" Captain Butch Todd. I retired from the U.S.A.F. a few years ago, and I have been summoned by General Brown, along with my assistant detective, Claire Cavendish. I'm not exactly sure why we are here." Butch thought he had said enough and waited to see how the colonel would address his clarification of his current civilian status.

"The general will see you as soon as he is free. He is currently on a very important telephone conference which is related to your mission while you are here. Please make yourself comfortable in those chairs, and I will alert the general that you are waiting." The colonel left them, did not acknowledge any clarification that Butch had hoped to relay to the general, and then disappeared through a door that was most likely the general's personal space. In less than five minutes, the colonel returned to the room and informed them that he was taking them to the general's personal office. He turned on his heel in a distinct military fashion and marched them into the general office. The colonel stood at attention in front of the oversized desk which the general was sitting behind, saluted his superior, announced Butch and Claire, and turned and left them alone with General Brown.

The general motioned for them to sit in the two uncomfortable straight back chairs that fronted his desk, then he opened a file, leafed through several pieces of official looking documents, and shut the folder before he spoke to his guests.

"I'm going to address you two as Butch and Claire. You may address me as General," he said. "We have a quandary on our hands, Butch, and of all the active and retired U.S.A.F. officers whom we think we can trust, you are number one on our list. I brought you and Claire to the Pentagon today to impress upon both of you that we are contemplating that we may have a National Security crisis on our hands." He stopped speaking and looked at his guests to see if he had captured their interest. They were staring at him, waiting for the other shoe to drop.

"I can understand why you would be concerned, General. A multi-million-dollar aircraft, the crew, and untold secrets going down in flames for no apparent reason would make any leader of our military very upset. What I don't understand is why with all the O.S.I. investigators, top-secret agents on the government payroll, and the finest trained jet pilots in the world at your beck and call, you would choose a retired military junior officer to investigate for you," Butch said. The O.S.I. was the Office for Special

Intelligence department, an equivalent of the C.I.D. for the U.S. Army, and the NCIS department for the U.S. Navy. All these agencies were designed to work independently of the chain of command in each branch of the service, reporting their findings directly to a committee at the Pentagon.

"That's exactly why I called on you." The general let that simmer in the air for a minute before adding. "We don't know if there is a leak in the Pentagon, the O.S.I., or somewhere else, but as you know having flown military aircraft, it is very, very rare for one of our birds to go down unexpectedly without the suspicion of hostile fire or sabotage. Do you agree?" Butch thought for a moment before he answered.

"I can see your point, by why me? I'm just a retired captain, and I don't hold a rank high enough to upset anyone's apple cart." The general opened up his desk drawer, took out some papers, a small box, and a fountain pen. He pushed the papers over to Butch to read and sign. Butch read them, looked up astonished at the general, and immediately signed the papers without further questions.

"You are now Colonel Butch Todd, Special Investigator for the O.S.I., reporting only to me at the Pentagon. Your assistant will carry the same authority as yourself, however, without a commission. You will be paid at the 0-6 commission level while you are assigned to this duty. Upon completing your mission, whether you succeed or fail, you will be immediately retired again, but this time as a colonel in the U.S.A.F., with all the benefits that accompany such a rank. Do you have any other questions?" Butch shook his head indicating that he did not have more questions, and the general began to outline the job duties Butch would be performing. Before launching into the description of his job duties, the general picked up his telephone desk set, called Colonel Summers into his office, and they waited for his appearance. The colonel brought in an OCP uniform with colonel insignias embroidered on each shoulder, and an embroidered name on the uniform with the last name Todd clearly attached to the upper left-hand side of the uniform. The general then slid a pair of bright silver eagle insignias in the box that he was holding over to Butch.

"You now have uniform privileges in the BX on any U.S.A.F. base. You are being given and unlimited clothing allowance for you and your assistant so you can dress accordingly and "fit in" on any military installation you may need to visit. We will not be commissioning Claire, but we will give her a temporary rank of Special Investigator, which will come with a badge and an identification card. Your personal military rank and officer's credentials should open any doors you need while on active duty. If anyone, other than the President or Vice-President should question your authority or try to impede your investigation, you will simply pick up this Sat phone and call Colonel Summers. That should be the end of any roadblock you may encounter. Any questions?"

"Not at this time, General. When do we begin our investigation?"

"As soon as you are briefed on the information that we know at this time. Colonel Summers will brief you and Claire before you leave the Pentagon today. We will need a few hours to put everything into play that I have suggested to you. Please step into my private head and try on your uniform. We think it should fit you fine. I need to speak to Claire for a moment anyway, and that will let us accomplish both tasks." Butch stood, reached for the uniform that Colonel Summers was still holding, and went into the general's private bathroom to change.

"Claire, I am glad that Butch has encouraged you to join him in his endeavor. Butch has taken an oath to this country and the U.S.A.F. of loyalty and commitment. I am going to read the same oath to you. If you agree with what you hear, simply state I do, and you will be a sworn private agent for the U.S.A.F."

"Certainly, Sir."

"Please repeat after me: "I, Clair Cavendish, do solemnly agree to uphold the laws of the United States Constitution, the U.S.A.F., and any other laws that govern the regions of the country for which I am assigned. I further agree to uphold the principles of the U.S. Code of Conduct for military personnel and understand that my failure to do so could result in my prosecution in a military court of law." She repeated the oath, the general slid her identification card and badge across the desk to her, and she quietly put them into her purse. Butch returned from the general's head dressed in his camo outfit, and he looked as if he could still fly jet attack bombers if the need arose. Butch and Claire were ready to receive the briefing from Colonel Summers, and they would immediately be submerged into an investigation that neither of them would ever forget.

Chapter 4

Unanswered Questions

The briefing by Colonel Summers was anything but brief. After leaving General Brown's office, Colonel Summers walked Butch and Claire to the security elevator, where they had to be checked again with a security wand, and all three entered the elevator for a destination unknown to Butch and Claire. Summers pressed a button on the elevator panel, and the car began to move quickly downward. Butch and Claire saw the floor numbers decrease from five to four, four to three, and so on, until they saw the numbers on the panel turn red, and the floors were identified with capital letters. When the elevator stopped at level C, Summers asked them to follow him down a corridor that was dimly lit and appeared totally abandoned, except for the three of them. Summers walked them to a door with no windows, opened it with an electronic key, and ushered them inside, offering them chairs that faced a gigantic flat-screen television that had a static picture of the United States White House showing as a backdrop.

Colonel Summers picked up a wall telephone unit, spoke something softly into the phone, and placed the receiver back on the wall unit. Almost immediately the large television screen came to life with an image of the Oval Office in the background. Claire looked at Butch with more questions than answers in her stare, but before she could ask Butch a question, three men walked into the room, one positioning himself in front of the desk, one sitting to the side of the desk, and the last one sitting *behind* the desk. Butch had to do a doubletake before he was convinced that he was seeing what he thought he was seeing—the President of the United States, along with his Chief of Staff, and his personal assistant.

Butch looked over at Claire and she had a big grin on her face. She whispered in jest to Butch, but the room had obviously been wired for surveillance because the question she had asked Burch was answered by POTUS.

"Yes, Special Agent Cavendish, I am the President of the United States. Officially, my name is Ronaldo Eugene White, III, but you can just call me Mr. President." There was no smile on his face, so Claire was shocked into the reality of the moment.

"Good morning, Mr. President," Claire said softly.

"Good morning to both of you. Let's get to the matter which caused you to be recruited, and I will have my Chief of Staff, General Andrew Cooper, fill you in on what we currently know, and what we need to know going forward. General Cooper?"

"Yes, Mr. President. First, what I am about to tell you is top secret, cryptographic, eyes-only, classified information that you must protect at all costs. Under no circumstances are you to share anything related to this case to anyone other than the four people in this office and in your room at the Pentagon. Is that clear?"

"Yes, Sir," both Butch and Claire answered quickly.

"I am going to give you the background information that we currently believe to be true, and I will also share with you our beliefs about why we are concerned about the exposure we have experienced with the crash of Flight C5-SGM12. First, although the report that was made about the crash of Flight C5-SGM12 was technically true, we intentionally omitted some information that was highly classified in our public reporting. Second, we have reason to believe that espionage or blackmail was a mitigating factor in the loss of the jet and the eight military personnel who were killed in the crash. While it is not impossible for a military aircraft to experience mechanical issues which could force a pilot to bring the bird down unexpectedly, we have recovered the Black Box from the crash site and there was no indication from the data recorders that anything like that happened with Flight C5-SGM12. Autopsies have been performed on all eight of the bodies that we recovered from the wreckage of the jet, and we have some abnormalities that indicate that foul play was an issue with the circumstances of the crash of the airliner. At this time, that is all I am prepared to share with you." The general paused, drank from a bottle of water, and then continued.

"We need both a detective and a master jet qualified pilot to investigate this incident. We have Special Ops people who can investigate, and we have qualified pilots who can accurately predict what may have happened at 35,000 feet to bring this bird down, but, unfortunately, we need someone who can do both tasks at the same time. With that in mind, I will ask you and Special Agent Cavendish a simple question. Do you believe that you can honestly take on this assignment, work completely undercover, and help us solve his dilemma? The security of the nation may rest upon your findings."

Butch looked at Claire, she nodded positively on her willingness to serve her country in this investigation, and then Butch directed his next question to POTUS.

"Mr. President, I have a couple of questions that I need answered from either you or General White unequivocally before I can commit myself and my associate to this mission. Would you prefer I address the general or you?" One could hear a pin drop in the room after Butch asked his question. No one, and I mean *no one*, ever called the President of the United States out to answer such a question. Collin Blackmon, the Administrative Assistant to the President, began to speak but POTUS cut him off in mid-sentence.

"Colonel Todd," POTUS began to address in Butch in almost a familial way, "I have been completely briefed on your experience as an active U.S.A.F. combat pilot, your reasons for leaving the service, and your career as a private investigator, and now the City of Ashburn, Alabama, Police Chief. While that doesn't mean you have 'reinvented the wheel,' or anything as dramatic as that, you have displayed an uncanny ability to solve problems in a prudent and timely fashion. That doesn't mean that you and your assistant will solve our problem quickly, or possibly at all, but you are the kind of person I want getting to the bottom of this crisis. While the official report is that the pilot of Flight C5-SGM12 possibly took his own life, and those other seven aviators with him, I want to know the unadulterated truth. We have some evidence that indicates that a foreign entity may have been complicit in the crash, and having been a combat pilot in Afghanistan, you know the importance of knowing the truth about your enemy. As terrible as 'suicide by jet crash' might be to the morale of our country's military forces, espionage or other interactions by foreign governments is far worse. Closing our eyes to such a potential truth and thinking it will go away is not a course of action I intend to approve. Do you understand me, Colonel?" POTUS had not really raised his voice, but he had emphasized the importance of this mission, and why he believed that Butch was just the right man for the job.

"Yes, Mr. President, I do understand your concern. My question to you is simply this. If Claire and I discover espionage, subterfuge, or some other egregious criminal activity that may have a negative effect upon the U.S. Government or its people, will our findings be swept under the rug or discounted as unfounded or non-existent? That would be the only reason I would believe I could not serve you and my country in the task you have outlined for me." Butch said nothing, General Cooper was quiet, and Collin Blackmon was flabbergasted that a commissioned officer in the U.S.A.F. would even pose such a question to his Commander-in-Chief. However, POTUS just began to smile and nod his head.

"Excellent, Colonel Todd. Great question, and one I will answer unequivocally. If you and Special Agent Cavendish discover any kind of deceit or subterfuge that can be proven beyond a reasonable doubt, I will personally guarantee you in front of these witnesses that he or she will meet the full fury of the wrath of the United States of America. I cannot promise you that such a person will be publicly tried in a court of law, because we have to consider the National Security implication of every action we take. However, whether it be Guantanamo, or some other secure prison, anyone who is proven to have caused irreparable harm to this country will be imprisoned until a fair trial is conducted as to their guilt or innocence. If found guilty, they will either receive a life sentence in a secure location, or they may be executed by a firing squad. The U.S. Attorney General will determine the punishment of such a person if such results require his involvement. In other words, Colonel, I want this person to pay for the lives of eight U.S.A.F. soldiers, and a $268 Million dollar jet airplane. Does that answer your questions about our intent?"

"Yes, Sir. I wholeheartedly accept that commission, Mr. President."

"Thank you for your service, Colonel Todd, and yours as well, Special Agent Cavendish. Please keep me informed through official channels with General Brown's office." The huge television screen went black, the lights in the room came up to a normal setting, and Colonel Summers looked at Butch differently than when he had walked them into the secret meeting room.

"I'll say one thing for you, Colonel Todd. You have guts!" Colonel Summers walked them back to the elevator, pressed the lobby button, and escorted Butch and Claire out of the building and into the clearing where the heliport had dropped them off a little earlier. Butch heard a chopper coming landing, and they were soon again aboard the military helicopter on their way back to the Joint Base Anacostia. They were whisked away to the G700 jet and flown back to Birmingham. As they were walking back to Butch's truck, Claire looked at him and shook her head.

"I know I can't tell anyone what just happened, but no one would believe you confronted the most powerful many in the free world just a few hours ago. You are something, Butch Todd."

"Something good or something bad?" he teased.

"Just something!"

* * *

The G700 landed safely at the 117th Wing of the Alabama National Guard in Birmingham with the sun sinking in the west. It was hard to believe that all this had taken place in less than twelve hours from when it had begun this morning. Had Butch or Claire had any knowledge beforehand that they would be having a one-on-one conversation with the most powerful man in the free world, they might have been less prepared than by the stark reality that their confrontation with POTUS would tilt their opinion of the mission toward the government's way. It just wasn't something that was done on a daily basis—it was refreshing, yet almost impossible to fathom. Butch and Claire now had to put a clear and concise plan together to accomplish the goals that POTUS had laid out for them—find the reason for the crash of Flight C5-SGM12, treason or suicide.

"Butch, I'm not sure what has happened since we boarded the G700 this morning, but I want to recap what I think and run it by you for comment. Is that acceptable to you?"

"Sure, but I'm not promising that I have any clearer a picture of the reality of things than you have."

"Assuming that you were selected for this mission because of your experience with military jets, along with your success as a private investigator, and I was included because General Brown wanted you to have a confidant to bounce your ideas off during your investigation, what do they really think you and I will discover that will give them a clear picture of what happened with that mammoth jet? What can we find or deduce that the NTSB or the Special Ops have not turned up in their internal investigation? Don't you find it a little odd that the U.S. Government, all the way to POTUS, is depending on a couple of civilians to do what their vaunted security services can't do—find a clue as to why the crash really happened?"

"Don't be too quick to sell us short, Claire. Since you have never served in the U.S. Military in a combat role, you are assuming things that may not be totally true. The information that is released to the general public is always filters though several layers of security scrutiny before we see headlines in the newspaper or hear the stories on cable news or Talk Radio. That's just the self-preservation tactics that the U.S. Government has taken since 1901, when President Theodore Roosevelt was the first POTUS given special protection by the U.S. Secret Service. Also, you must remember that if there is a conspiracy afoot, especially one that could have lasting ramifications on an enemy nation who may be complicit in the crash of Flight C5-SGM12, that any resulting news releases could be devasting to the security of this country. That's how WWI and WWII got started. We didn't start either one, but we were sucked into them because of our status in the world and because it was in the overall best interest of the United States to fight the Germans and Italians on foreign soil rather than waiting to defend our own soil at a later time. Geopolitical matters today are so sensitive that one false step, one move in the wrong direction, can cause the administration of POTUS, or even the entire U.S. Government, to fail. I think the President is very wise in his approach to this issue. We are bound as employees of the U.S. Government, as well as private investigator, to securing the truth and preserving the results. The only people we can share our findings with is the U.S. Government—in other words, POTUS. Sure, he could have found a more qualified pilot than me, or a more experienced investigative team than you and me, but if you look at things from a logical approach, we are the perfect tool for POTUS to use to reach his ultimate goals."

"Now that's what I call a good opinion of oneself!" Claire laughed. "You really think that POTUS has thought through all of that in regard to us—to you and me personally? I find that rather daunting and unbelievable!"

"Oh, contraire, Claire. POTUS doesn't do any research on his own. I'm sure ten minutes before he decided that we would be perfect for his exercise in discovering the truth, he didn't know our names or care that we even existed. However, he has 'people' to do that kind of thing for him. He has advisors who create multiple scenarios and present them to him on a daily basis. While he is trying to decide the best way to deal with a little fat tyrant in North Korea, or a dictator for life in China, something like the crash of the C5 plane arises. Normally, nothing of this sort would reach his decision level, but something tells me that we are not being told the full story here. What you and I need to know is 'why' the mission was being flown, and 'who' knew about it and its ultimate mission goals. We can't begin to solve a puzzle like this with so many pieces of the picture missing. That's why POTUS needed a private investigator who might push the legal limits of authority to achieve the results that he believes is out there and that must be uncovered."

"So, someone told POTUS, or his handlers, that you are capable of pushing back against authority when you believe it's necessary to discovering the truth? How could they know that about you? Granted, I believe you are the perfect investigator for such a mission, but how would someone 750 miles away know that about you?"

"Big Brother?" Butch smiled as he answered.

"Help me understand why they would even care that you are a wild card in such an investigation? Where is the logic of bringing in an outside at a time of such concern for National Security?"

"Two words, Claire. 'Plausible deniability.' That's all you need to know. Of course, they must think we can eventually uncover the truth, or they would not have gone to as much trouble as they have to make things happen for us to proceed as the primary investigators. However, in the end, they have to have plausible deniability to make sure their backsides are covered in case we are exposed by the media or someone who is determined to expose the U.S. Government in an unauthorized investigation."

"Now you're saying that we may be involved in an unauthorized investigation. Who is higher on the food chain is the U.S. Government than POTUS? That should make our investigation gold!"

"Claire, you may be forgetting that we have no idea where our investigation may take us. As a matter of law, the U.S. Government cannot investigate civilians without first notifying them of their Constitutional Rights of the 4th and 14th

Amendments to the U.S. Constitution. It all falls under the protection of a citizen against unlawful search and seizure by their government."

"And they believe we may be inclined to be blind to such considerations as we search for the truth?"

"Maybe. I can't say for sure. What I can say is that you have an option at this point of backing out of this investigation if you are uncomfortable in its scope and possible implications of impropriety. I will understand."

"But *you* will not back down—no way, no how, under no conditions? Right?"

"That's pretty much true. I'm not going to murder someone just because POTUS wants this case solved. I have every intention of keeping the Code of Conduct that I have been sworn to as an officer of the U.S.A.F., as well as my private investigator's code of conduct intact. If you are asking me if I will pursue a matter that leans into gray areas of the law, I cannot promise you anything at this time. You will either have to trust me or go your own way. Either way, I will understand and not hold it against you. I know what I intend to do, but I can't instruct you to do likewise."

"You're not getting rid of me that easily," she laughed. "I just wanted to know the ground rules."

"Basically, the ground rules are that we make them up as we go along, trying not to infringe too much upon the rights of any particular individual who might be affected along the way. Claire, this investigation could prevent WWIII, or something worse. I can't walk away from my country when she calls me out for help."

"What could be worse than WWIII?"

"Let's hope we never find out!"

Chapter 5

The Plan

Butch drove he and Claire home from the Birmingham National Guard hangar with a gigantic burden on his conscious. The very last thing that he wanted to happen to him at this phase of his life was to get involved in something so sinister that he could not even talk about it to a priest. He also worried about having dragged Claire into an investigation of such great magnitude this early in her investigative career. She had had a small success or two since joining up with him as his assistant investigator for the Ashburn City Police Department, but she had not been in a live-or-die situation before—a dogfight in the sky in a multi-million-dollar jet with enough armaments to level an average sized American city. He had had to be able to react, not think about what actions he would take if an enemy MIG-29 decided to shoot him out of the sky. There were evasive actions, counteractions, and eventually kill options that Butch would employ in a matter of seconds to insure his own existence. Butch didn't have the time or inclination to teach Claire about survival techniques that came naturally to him after his years of combat duty in the U.S.A.F. Yet, he had made her vulnerable to their current mission, and now he felt responsible to look out for her best interests. It was an added burden that he really didn't need under the circumstances.

"Your mind seems to be somewhere in the stratosphere, Butch. What are you thinking?" How could he tell her that he was worried that she would be more of a liability than an asset as they tackled one of the most dangerous missions of his career?

"Just trying to take it all in, Claire. We have a daunting task ahead of us and I'm not sure how to approach it yet. I just have a lot on my mind."

"Let me see if I can help you. In the past you were the captain of the aircraft, the indisputable conquering hero for your country, and you needed no one to help you shoot down enemy aircraft or drop bombs on the forces of evil. Now, all of a sudden, you have a co-pilot. Someone who is not as qualified as you or as experienced in conflict as you, and you aren't sure that 'babysitting' an assistant is such a good thing. How am I doing?" Butch had always known that musicians and artist were more sensitive to things going on around them, but this was eerie. How could Claire have picked up on his concerns about her so quickly?"

"It's not like that, Claire. I'm just accustomed to working on my own when dangerous missions are involved, and I don't want to put you in a compromised position and endanger your life. It's a big responsibility."

"Tell me how this case differs from the murder of innocents on a university campus by a crazed competing instructor who wanted the murdered professor's job? Could I have been injured or killed in that investigation?" She waited for Butch to answer.

"That's not the point."

"Really? What is the point. Dead is dead, or at least it was the last time I checked. Butch, no one can determine what will happen in an investigation of any type, much less one of National Security concerns. What you really should be asking yourself are the following questions: Can Claire shoot straight and true; is Claire as smart now as she was a few weeks ago when we solved an impossibly difficult crime; and do I trust her to have my back? Those are the only things that matter right now."

"I'd have to agree with all three of your questions, were I asked to tell the truth about my feelings for your loyalty and abilities. However, the U.S. Military plays by different rules than the civilian courts of law. Just because we find the truth and turn our findings over to those in command, that doesn't assure us that we will be exonerated in our successful solving of this case. What I'm suggesting is that you have to be on board with the possibility that we may be used as sacrificial lambs for the U.S.A.F., or POTUS himself, assuming they want to write a different ending to our story than what it really turns out to be. Can you agree with those terms?"

"Can you?" Butch thought for a minute and smiled. Claire had turned the tables on him, and now he had to admit that if he were willing to put his reputation and life on the line for his country, he had no right to refuse Claire the same opportunity.

"So, we're good with our decision to move forward with this case?"

"Absolutely. Now, get us home so I can get a Jacuzzi and wash my hair!"

"Will you need a backrub to go along with the bath?"

"One never knows."

* * *

Butch and Claire spent some quality time together in the Jacuzzi, and afterward in the bedroom, and it wasn't about quality sleep time. While they were attracted to each other sexually, they might go several days or more than a week before sharing a Jacuzzi or a night of frolic in the bedroom. It had been an exhausting trip for both of them, and between the jetlag and the increased pressure exerted upon them after visiting with POTUS, they just needed to unwind. They both fell asleep as soon as their heads touched their pillows that evening, and Butch told Claire that the first act on their agenda in the morning was to put together a logical, achievable plan to accomplish their overall goals. He wasn't sure how that would happen, but he was too tired to work through things in his mind that night. Hopefully, a good night's rest, and a new day with new possibilities would clarify things for them tomorrow.

Butch heard the shower running and he thought he was still dreaming. He had relived their visit to the Pentagon and their encounter with POTUS in his most vivid dreams all night after their previous day's journey to the Pentagon. He faintly heard a woman's voice asking him if he intended to get up and go to work or not. Coming out of his mental fog, Butch saw Claire standing at the foot of the bed, her hair wrapped in a large white towel, and another large towel wrapped around her petite frame.

"Why don't we stay in today, take a day off, and have a little R&R (rest and recuperation)?" R&R was allotted to mIlItary personnel in combat zones and hardship assignments, and Butch evidently thought he had earned such a break after flying to Maryland and meeting with General Brown. Claire was not so understanding.

"What a wimp!" she said and pulled the covers off his naked body as he still lay in the bed. "*Colonel*, it is Colonel Todd, right? I don't think your promotion came with a vacation. Rather, my perception of our visit with General Brown and POTUS was that we were to get to work without delay determining what really happened to Flight C5-SGM12. Was I mistaken?" Claire asked the obvious question.

"Spoil sport!" Butch said as he got up and walked to the shower. "I'll have some coffee if you're a mind to bring me a cup in the bathroom."

"Do I look like a waitress or your 'main squeeze?' You need to make yourself presentable so we can plan our next move. I'll set you out a cup of coffee and scramble you a couple of eggs, but the party is over for now. You will need to earn my companionship going forward."

Butch came out of the bathroom to find Claire had dressed casually in a jump suit and tennis shoes. She had their breakfast on the small table in the apartment, and they sat down with the newspaper to begin the serious portion of their day. Butch pointed out a headline in the *Ashburn Times*, asking Claire what she thought of the statement.

"I would say that the changes made to accommodate Mayor Hannity did not go unnoticed by the staff at the local newspaper." Of course, anyone who dressed the part of a perfectly presentable military person in Ashburn, Alabama, would turn many heads. The story above the fold on the first page of the *Ashburn Times* was about the new police personnel standing in for Chief Butch Todd and Detective Claire Cavendish, complete with pictures of the two new helpers. Butch thought they looked exactly as whom they were—military police in civilian clothes on guard duty in a small Southern town. The story didn't relate any details because no details had been forthcoming to anyone in town, with the exception of Mayor Hannity, Sally Lancaster, the mayor's secretary, and Butch and Claire themselves. The mayor had decided that it would be better for people to wonder about the temporary hired guns than to try and explain their existence. Anyway, Claire and Butch were on a secret mission that the mayor had little or no information about, so he couldn't have shared the story even if he had wanted to do so.

"Nice looking guys," Claire said as she looked at the young men in their starched and pressed suits. "They don't even look real!" She was admiring their appearance when Butch said, "They're real—very real. What we need to do is focus on our next move and not worry about the two dreamy, young men standing in for us!"

"Are you jealous that I might find them handsome and attractive?"

"No, I'm concerned that we need to focus on our task at hand. Now, where were we last night before we decided to celebrate our mission to D.C. and return?"

"Let's eat first, and after I clear the table, we can begin to devise a plan. I think we need to be in Charleston, S.C., as soon as possible before any remaining leads to the crash evaporate into the sky, or wherever leads go when they are lost to the detectives working the case."

"I agree with the Charleston temporary residence for this investigation. We have a blank check, as far as housing, food, and other expenses are concerned, so I have taken the liberty of booking us a couple of rooms in the Gaslight Inn on Meeting Street. Historic Downtown Charleston is only a few miles from Joint Base Charleston and the Charleston International Airport. We can rent a car and be in the Historic District in a matter of twenty minutes or so."

"Charleston International Airport? Really? Besides London, England, with stops along the way, where outside of the United States continent do flights originate or their destinations end internationally from CIA?"

"Well, London *is* an international city. What's your problem?"

"I just have always taken issue with small regional airports in medium sized cities claiming that their regional airport is an *international* one."

"Technically speaking, Claire, it only takes one flight to Bermuda, the Bahamas, or Cancun, Mexico, to make any airport international in scope. Why do we care if they call themselves international if they only fly to Podunk, Illinois?"

"Just an observation, Butch. That is what we have been hired to do, is it not? Observe and report back to POTUS?" Claire was picking at Butch the only way she knew that would get under his skin.

"Fine," he said. "As I was saying, we will fly into Charleston *International* Airport on a commercial flight, take a taxi or Uber to the Gaslight Inn, and begin putting our plan into action once we are on the ground in Charleston. I know the Innkeeper personally, and I'll get him to take one of their rooms and set us up an office near our sleeping rooms. That way we can work into the night without causing suspicion among the local folks."

"I've only been to Charleston once in my past, and it was to perform at the Dock Street Theatre. It seemed like a nice town, with some fantastic restaurants within walking distance of the Historic District."

"For many years Charleston had one of the best culinary schools in the world operating in the Historic District. Johnson & Wales University was located in North Charleston for many years and some of the finest chefs ever to wield a spoon were graduates of that fine institution. It didn't really matter which of the restaurants you visited when in Charleston, because almost all of them were Johnson & Wales graduate chefs."

"You said it *was* in Charleston. Is it no longer there? If so, why did it disappear?"

"Johnson & Wales is a nationally recognized chef school second to none in the United States. It began in Providence, Rhode Island, in 1914, and it expanded into several cities by establishing two and four-year programs for the purpose of teaching the best in culinary techniques to local students who wanted to become some of the world's most successful chefs. In 1986, Johnson & Wales established a school in Charleston, S.C., and the school and the local restaurants flourished for more than twenty years while it operated in the Low Country. However, in 2006 J&W decided to consolidate their institutions of learning and relocated several regional schools to Charlotte, N.C. That was the death knell for the finest restaurants in Charleston, in my opinion. There is still a culinary school in Charleston, but it will never be the same."

"Are we going there to eat, or is our mission to determine what happened to Flight C5-SGM12?" Claire loved to ask redundant questions that made Butch realized that he sometimes lost focus on the mission they were undertaking.

"Both," he smiled. "One does not go to Charleston and stay at the Holiday Inn and eat at McDonalds! No, no, no! A trip to Charleston is not complete unless one stays at the Gaslight Inn on Meeting Street and Market, has brunch at 82 Queen Restaurant, and a fine dinner of crispy flounder at Anson's on Market Street."

"You're serious, aren't you?" she said in amazement. It appeared to Claire that Butch's first mission was where to stay and eat in Charleston, and the discovery of the details of the crash of a $248 million aircraft was secondary.

"Oh, yes, Claire. I will teach you about Charleston while we solve the mystery of the crash of Flight C5-SGM12.

Charleston has much to teach you about style, grace, and charm while we are working for Uncle Sam—350 years of Southern style for a start."

"That sounds great, but don't you think we should put a comprehensive plan together before we leave Birmingham? I wouldn't want to get sidetracked by all the talk of food and historic places!"

"Laugh if you want, but before our mission is over you will admit that I was 100% correct about the charm of Charleston, South Carolina!"

* * *

After breakfast, Butch and Claire got to work laying out an overall strategy to the best of their abilities. When beginning a sophisticated approach to problem solving, Butch knew that one first had to start with the facts that were known, and then through research and deductive reasoning more clues would point the way to the ultimate solution to the problem. This is the methodology that they employed in the case of the crash of Flight C5-SGM12.

"So, what do we know, Claire, about the crash of Flight C5-SGM12? I mean, what do we *really* know from what we speculate that we might know?"

"The big bird crashed," was all Claire answered.

"Good, good, Claire. Don't move to fast so I can keep up!" he said and chuckled at her simplicity.

"Actually, Butch, that is all that we know at this point in time, sitting in our apartment in Ashburn, Alabama, five hundred miles west of Joint Base Charleston. Everything else is pure speculation from that fact forward."

"Agreed. I was looking over the documentation that Colonel Summers provided us when we visited at the Pentagon about the crash, and there are a few other things that we can add to that ultimate fact that the C5A crashed. All of the bodies were recovered at the crash scene, or at least enough of the bodies which provided the Office of the Armed Forces Medical Examiner (OAFME), to draw certain conclusions."

"I have my pen and legal pad ready. How shall we list the information you are about to share with me?"

"Let's go by name, rank, cause of death, time of death, and any unusual circumstances surrounding any of the deaths recorded at the scene of the crash site."

"I'm ready, but I do have a question. Do you think you will find C.O.D. or T.O.D. different on any of the eight servicemen pronounced dead at the scene of the crash? That would appear unusual, would you not agree?"

"I would agree, so let's see what the official report says. We can't assume anything at this point of the investigation. Two pilots, six crew personnel, and specific autopsy reports for each of them. I believe we can trust the OAFME's results, don't you?"

"Of course. I guess the crash site analytics is as good a place to start as any."

They went through the report, starting with the least ranking service person, Airman Jonathan Holder, to the highest-ranking officer on board, Lt. Colonel Ralph McGee, the commander of Flight C5-SGM12. The findings were consistent until they reached the pilot and the co-pilot of the large aircraft. While the T.O.D. of each of the members of Flight C5-SGM12 was identical, the C.O.D. was questionable in both flight officers."

"Now that's something I didn't think I would find," Butch remarked as he read the C.O.D. of Lt. Colonel McGee and Major Buddy Hawkins, the co-pilot of the flight. Butch's remark got Claire's full attention, and she began to speculate immediately on what the C.O.D. might mean.

"How could there be a different C.O.D. with the two pilots? They all went down together in a fiery crash, didn't they?"

"According to the OAFME, Major Hawkins had high levels of narcotics in his blood results, while Lt. Colonel McGee had elevated levels of sarin in his blood work. Sarin is a favorite poison employed by the Russians when they want to eliminate a problem citizen or competitor."

"What kind of narcotic was in the major's bloodstream?"

"That hasn't been determined at this time, according to the autopsy report, but the question we need to answer is whether the major was complicit in the crash of Flight C5-SGM12 or just another victim."

"I can see why General Brown and POTUS are involved in this investigation. If it is proven that the Soviets caused the flight crew of C5-SGM12 to be poisoned, it could be interpreted as a blatant and overt act of war against the United States. I think my worry index just leaped beyond its normal limits."

"Claire, I knew there was a reason why I was selected to head this investigation. Now it is becoming even clearer to me."

"How about sharing your clarity, Partner? I'm still in the dark."

"One of the things that I have been sworn to secrecy about my past military career has to do with a short stint I spent in an Afghanistan confinement camp. I guess I can share that information with you since we are in this thing together."

"Thanks for the confidence," she mocked.

"Seriously, I was captured with several non-combatants when I was serving in Afghanistan and was taken to a camp outside the city of Kabul. The locals had turned us over to the rebels and we were to be used as pawns to negotiate some kind of prisoner swap or some other action to benefit the rebels. I had been in a secret club trying to infiltrate the Afghanistan rebels when we were raided by the local militia. As you may be aware, there is no tolerance for the consumption of alcohol at any age in many of the Islamic cities, and Afghanistan was at the top of that list. There were several other American and British civilians partaking of the sins of alcohol and loose women, and I was there to learn more about an area that the Allies would be bombing in the coming week. Fortunately, it was assumed that I was nothing but a stupid American, and I was released when the U.S. Embassy in Kabul interceded for us. We were released, I made it back to my unit, and I used the intelligence that I learned that night to pinpoint where to make our strike in my warbird."

"Interesting story, Butch, but how does that put you in a special place to be selected by the U.S.A.F. Chief of Staff and POTUS to become the principal investigator in this crash? Something was lost to me in the translation of your story."

"While at the club, and then again at the detention camp outside of Kabul, I overhead that the Russians were planning to use poison to regain control of the Afghanistan government, and that sarin was the poison of choice. They spoke of where the supply was being hidden, and one of my missions shortly after being released into the custody of the American Embassy was to lead a group of F-111B fighter bombers against that facility and destroy it completely. Maybe the general and POTUS just felt comfortable using someone who had prior knowledge of Russian techniques in eliminating their enemies. That's all I can figure at this time."

"Were you debriefed, as I think you call it, when you returned from being captured?"

"Yes, we were all questioned by the CIA and released back to our units. I was sworn to secrecy about what I had overheard, and I never thought about it again. That was three years before I retired from the U.S.A.F., so I would be amazed if that had anything to do with our assignment."

"The government has a long memory, Butch. Never forget that."

"Don't worry. I will *never* forget anything about my service time with the U.S.A.F. However, let's plan an overall approach to this task and work out the details as we learn more facts once we're in Charleston."

"Good idea. I think our first step in the plan is knowing what to pack for dinner at Anson's!"

Chapter 6

The Gaslight Inn

Butch and Claire flew into the Charleston International Airport on an overcast Monday morning, feeling the bumpy humid air tossing the small jetliner all around the skies until it landed safely and taxied down the tarmac to the terminal area. They flew directly from the National Guard's 117th Wing detachment in Birmingham to the public airport in Charleston to prevent making a larger statement about their involvement in the investigation of Flight C5-SGM12 and its crew. Since the equipment they flew in on was not a commercial aircraft, they had to deplane on the runway and walk to the terminal to retrieve their baggage. Butch and Claire had been offered a staff car to pick them up and deliver them to their hotel in downtown Charleston, but Butch wanted to make this as low key an entrance into the city as possible. Also, Butch had to bring two wardrobes, a civilian one and his U.S.A.F. official uniform and its accoutrements for those times when he needed to make his military rank and presence known to positively influence those he needed help from in the investigation. For the most part, Butch wanted Claire and himself to operate under the radar of public opinion. Once they retained their luggage, they took a Hertz bus to the rental car parking lot and retrieved the sedan that Butch had set up for their use while they were in Charleston. It was a plain-Jane sedan, some General Motors model, with four doors and modest hubcaps, and no bells and whistles.

"Could you have picked out an uglier automobile, Butch? This has to be a four or five years old common sedan looking for a place to retire to the scrap heap."

"I told the rental agent that I wanted a safe, unnoticeable, four door sedan, that while reliable, would not draw attention to us as we did our jobs in Charleston. I think he reserved us the perfect ride."

"Remind me to never let you pick out what I am going to wear to dinner!" She laughed at her comment, but Butch knew she meant every word of it.

"Well it's too late for breakfast, and way too early for dinner, so we will simply have to go to 82 Queen for lunch, once we get settled into our rooms at the Gaslight Inn at Meeting Street and Market. We have only about a twenty-minute ride into the city and checking into the Gaslight Inn will be a breeze. Remember, I know the Innkeeper, Allen Johnson, personally." After having loaded their suitcases into the trunk of the sedan, Butch exited the Charleston International Airport area, entered I-26 South, and headed toward the Meeting Street exit into downtown Historic Charleston.

Historic Charleston was located at the end of the peninsula that was bounded by the Cooper River to the east, and the Ashley river to the west. In Colonial times and during the early development of the plantations that were responsible for making Charleston one of the wealthiest cities in the New World, the Cooper and Ashley rivers flowing to and from the Charleston Bay area was the principal means of transportation from the gigantic cotton and rice plantations that lay to the north of the city. Many a church service was interrupted before its ending if the tide was rising and the parishioners needed to get home to Middleton Place and Magnolia Gardens before the tide began falling again, bringing the water from upstream back into the harbor. Twelve-Oaks Plantation, Drayton Hall, and other plantations had also been constructed near Charleston in Antebellum South Carolina, but they could be reached by horse and buggy easier than Magnolia Plantation and Middleton

Place. At seventeen miles in distance, on gravel or mostly dirt roads, travel to Middleton Place by horse and buggy was a major undertaking in 1735, the year that Charleston was founded. Not until the gasoline engine and better roads were constructed was it feasible to travel to and from Historic Charleston faster than by boat up the Ashley River or to other points up the Cooper River. After the Civil War, those plantations that had not been burned by the Northern troops, were eventually made into museums and preserved as a testament to the wealth and ostentatious grandeur of the Old South.

"There's your exit," Claire said to Butch as they drove down I-26. The freeway veered to the left and a new intersection of I-526 and I-26 began that would route thru traffic around the city and southward to US Hwy 17, which would eventually connect with I-95, the freeway to Savannah and all points south. I-26 actually ended in the Battery portion of the old city, with only a couple of ways off the peninsula by way of elevated bridges over the Ashley River.

As Butch and Claire made their way down Meeting Street, the last exit off I-26 in downtown Charleston before the highway took a severe turn and became an elevated bridge over the Cooper River to the east, Butch watched Claire's expression as they slowly drove past historic buildings, fountains, and other points of interest which Butch had taken for granted all the many years that he had come here to enjoy the Southern hospitality and charm that this magnificent city. As Butch pulled into the loading zone in front of the Gaslight Inn, Claire looked up in delight.

"*This* is where we are going to stay during our investigation?"

"You don't like it," he teased.

"Like it? I love it. How old is this hotel? It looks like it was around during the Civil War."

"Let me begin by saying that South Carolina was founded in 1633 by eight English nobles with a Royal Charter from King Charles II. It remained a part of the Carolina colony, which it shared with North Carolina, until 1729 when it was declared the eighth state to ratify the U.S. Constitution in 1788. Because of the flourishing plantations that produced rice, cotton, and other consumables that were shipped directly to Europe from its port, Charleston became one of the most important trading partners of the New World with its European ancestors. It was ripe for the Yankees to target it because of its commerce, not just because of slavery."

"As to the history of this particular hotel, the current façade only dates back to 1980 when the Limehouse Family purchased the property and created a quality hotel for the visitors who come to Charleston. Prior to that time, this property began as a theatre in 1837, was totally destroyed by a fire that ravished the City of Charleston in 1861, then became a saloon, restaurant, and a wholesaler of German beers and Rhine wines. In later years, it was an auto parts store, dental equipment and supply store, liquor store, and bicycle rental company. However, in 1981 the current family that owns the property renovated it and it has been the Gaslight Inn for the past forty years! I don't think you will be disappointed in the ambiance or service provided by the Gaslight Inn." They instructed the valet to put their baggage on the rolling cart, and Butch and Claire entered the inn through the door that fronted Meeting Street. Allen spotted Butch immediately and offered a warm welcome.

"Butch! How good it is to see you again. I have reserved rooms 105, 106, and 108 for your pleasure while you reside with us. Do you have a target date of when you plan to leave, or do you want me to leave the reservation open-ended?"

"Let's leave it open for now. We are not sure exactly how long we plan to be here, but I imagine it may be for a couple of weeks. Let me introduce you to my assistant, Ms. Claire Cavendish. She is a recent graduate of Ashburn University in Cullman County, Alabama, and she and I are on an investigative mission here in Charleston."

"For the young lady's information, we have a turn-down service in the evenings around dinnertime, and we have wine and cocktails served on the patio from 4:00 PM until 6:00 PM, sometimes with music provided by local artists. Our complimentary breakfast can be brought to your room, or you may select what you want from the fresh fruit, muffins, and other delights provided in the lobby area, and take them to the patio and enjoy them with a complimentary newspaper. Did I miss anything?" Allen asked Butch when he had finished his spiel.

"Only that the hotel will make complimentary reservations for guests at local restaurants when requested, and that you have a wake-up call service. Oh, and I almost forgot, the best damn Jacuzzi in the city just outside our rooms!"

"I know how much you love to be at Jacuzzi level, so I made sure to block those rooms for you for your entire stay. If there is anything else we can do for you during your visit, please don't hesitate to ask."

"Would you please call Anson's and make us a reservation for two for dinner at 6:00 PM, or a seating close to that time? We will be out and about this afternoon, but we plan to return in plenty of time for dinner."

"Absolutely. I will have Anson's text the details to your phone when I have completed the reservations. Enjoy your stay." Butch nodded to Allen, Allen nodded to Claire, and they went to their rooms to prepare for lunch at 82 Queen.

Claire walked into room 105 and was blown away with the magnificence of the charming room, its authenticity of furniture, to include a canopied rice bed, and thick woven rugs covering heart pine floors. Referred to as the "King's wood" because of its durability and lasting value, heart pine flooring dated back to the log cabins constructed in the 1700s and 1800s. When the Gaslight Inn had been refurbished, Ms. Limehouse had spared no expense to make her hotel the best that Charleston could offer. Also, while the humidity in Charleston was often recorded at 80% and above, room 105 was cool and dry. The lace covered canopy bed tried to entice Claire to stretch out and enjoy the comforts of elegant rest, but she resisted. She opened her cosmetic bag, freshened her makeup, touched up her hair, and began to walk back down to the lobby. She saw Butch sitting on the other side of the Jacuzzi pool in an ornamental iron chair, taking in the sunshine and pleasant breezes that blew across the peninsula in the morning hours.

"Don't you look comfortable?" Claire called out. "Are you ready for lunch? By the way, are we going to take our car to the restaurant? I didn't see many places for parking along the streets."

"Oh, no. I had Allen have one of his valets park our car in their dedicated lot up the street. We will be walking most of the time we are in downtown Charleston. We will only use the car when we need to go to the Joint Base Charleston to begin our physical investigation of the crash."

"We are going to walk in this humidity. How far is 82 Queen?"

"Two blocks south down Meeting Street, and one block over west on Queen Street. It should take us less than ten minutes to make the stroll."

"Does 82 Queen have a colorful past like the Gaslight Inn?"

"They advertise that the building at 82 Queen Street is over 300 years old, and I wouldn't doubt that fact. The current restaurant that occupies the address is approximately thirty-five years old—it was begun sometime in the mid-1980s."

"Good food?"

"I'll let you tell me after we eat. The only advice I will offer is a few of their specialties on the menu. Of course, you can choose whatever you like. Remember, our Uncle Sam is paying the bill!" He smiled warmly at her and admired the pretty yellow sundress she had slipped on after arriving at the hotel.

"What are you getting?"

"82 Queen is famous for many things, but my favorite is their shrimp and grits, served with homemade bread. If we were on vacation, I'd suggest a light Chardonnay wine to top the meal off, but since we will be expensing our meals, it might not be a good idea to consume alcohol in the middle of the day."

"Excellent! I'll have that as well." The waiter came, took their order, brought them some sparkling water to sip while they were waiting on the chef to dazzle them with his culinary art, and Butch suddenly got very serious.

"Claire, I need to caution you before we get into this investigation waist deep. I have had dealings with the U.S. Government over the years, and I need to advise you to be on your guard the entire time we are employed by them to investigate the crash of Flight C5-SGM12. I'm not suggesting anything other than the truth is being sought by the U.S.A.F. and POTUS, but we need to cover our backsides in everything we do. People have been sacrificed and thrown under the bus for less than the truths we are trying to find."

"That warning sounds ominous. Should I be concerned about anything in particular?"

"No but stay alert. If something doesn't sound copesetic, it probably isn't. As much as possible we need to tape record our findings, interviews, and make specific notes about what we are being told and by whom. I didn't volunteer for this assignment because I had not had enough politicizing to last me the remaining years of my life. I didn't see any way to turn down POTUS or General Brown when asked to fulfill my duties as a retired U.S.A.F. officer and red-blooded American citizen. That doesn't mean that I don't intend to CYA. Understand?"

"Got it. You watch my six and I'll watch yours!"

"If you really want to know why I told the general that I needed your assistance was not for your expertise, which is good. I need to be able to trust whoever has my back, and that is you for me, and me for you!"

"I agree. By the way, have you had their chocolate cheesecake?" Claire was eyeing the dessert cart as it was rolled from table to table to the delight of those dining.

"No, but you can try it for both of us, if you wish to do so. I'm sure it only has a couple of thousand calories, hundreds of carbohydrates, and tons of processed sugars."

"You are really a bad man!" she said, chuckling as she had already decided that there was no way she wanted to tempt herself with such a sinful treat. "I'd like to be able to get into my clothes when I return to Ashburn, so I'll lay off the desserts while we're here." Butch called the waiter for the check, used his special credit card that General Brown's office had issued him for expenses, and gave the server a generous tip.

"Let's go back to our rooms, get dressed to go to the Joint Base Charleston, and see where we are in intelligence gathering at this point. I have a letter from General Brown that will open many doors for us, but if there are factors at work inside the base operations that may be complicit in the downing of Flight C5-SGM12, we need to know as much as we can before getting bogged down in details." Claire agreed, and they began the short walk back to the Gaslight Inn. As they walked by the Jacuzzi and observed couples playing in the bubbling water Claire shot a look at Butch that needed no interpretation. He just smiled in return.

Chapter 7

The Joint Base Charleston

Butch had Allen get one of his valets to retrieve the rental, and in a matter of minutes he and Claire were headed back up I-26 toward the Joint Base Charleston. In 1993, the Base Realignment and Closure Act (BRAC), accounted for the optimization of military bases by moving many of them under one command, thus eliminating much of the costs associated with so many independent locations. For instance, the United States Marine Corps, the 437th Airlift Wing, the 315th Airlift Wing, the 1st Combat Camera Squadron, the U.S. Army Corps of Engineers, and the Naval Information Warfare Center are all a part of the Joint Base Charleston operation. No one originally thought the U.S Marines, the U.S. Army, and the U.S.A.F. could coexist in one space before the realignment of the bases in 1993. With 67 military commands, 20,877 acres of land, and almost 80,000 service members of various branches of the U.S. Government operating in peaceful harmony at Joint Base Charleston, the impossible was happening. There were times when difficulty arose between the commands, but the D.O.D. (Department of Defense) maintained tight controls over the various factors at the base, and no irregularities between the branches of military service were tolerated. It was at this base, the 437th Airlift Wing of the U.S.A.F., where Colonel Ralph McGee and Major Buddy Hawkins had received their final briefing before Flight C5-SGM12 departed on a mission as yet not declassified by the U.S.A.F. If there were things to find that could shed some light upon the nature of the crash, Butch intended to find them. They pulled up to the gate of the base with Butch in full military uniform and with Claire in a proper business suit. Butch returned the salute of the sentry at the guard gate, watched as the airman look back and forth between the orders and the two people in the sedan, and eventually decided that everything was legitimate. He offered another salute, waved the sedan forward, and indicated to the gate operator to open the gate for the colonel's vehicle.

"Pretty tight security, don't you think?" Claire asked.

"I've seen tighter, but I've seen lighter as well. This is the outer most perimeter of a very secure military base. We will eventually have to get out of the car, walk through magnetometers, probably have a wand run over our bodies, and maybe even have a retina identification verified before we can get into the hangar where the remains of the C5 aircraft are being held."

"Do you think we will have barriers put in front of us that we cannot overcome?"

"No, and I now see why General Brown demanded that I be promoted to an 0-6 rank, full-bird colonel. Even with thousands of enlisted personnel and many officers in command here, there will only be one or two officers outranking me. It takes an admiral or general to pull rank on me, and with the accompanying letter that General Brown sent with us, I doubt anyone will want to account for obstructing our investigation."

"And I thought the military was so obtuse in these types of things," Claire said. She raised her eyebrows at Butch and gave him a little smile, letting him know that she was aware that they would be able to get the job done.

"I didn't come 500 miles to be told that I couldn't see the wreckage of the jet or examine all the records that have been assimilated to this point. What I don't understand is what other military intelligence the general and POTUS has to point them in the direction of the Russians. Anyone could have slipped poison into Colonel McGee's food or drink. Why suspect the Russians?"

"I think that's what we're here to discover. Let's just go about our work as we would if it were a civilian investigation and let the chips fall where they will."

"That's easy enough to say, but there are forces at work behind the scenes when something of this magnitude happens in one of the military branches that we have to discover. What we need to be looking for is what we cannot see!"

"Now that's going to be fun," Claire said. "I'll just put on my Captain Marvel glasses that I used when I was a kid to see the invisible!"

"You know what I mean, Claire. Each branch of the military has been trying to upstage each other branch since the inception of separate departments of defense came into existence. What I don't want to happen is for the truth to be buried because it may reveal that someone screwed up and let our military been infiltrated from outside the services. Saving face is the last thing I care about here. I want to know who is responsible for downing that $238 million dollar aircraft, and why he thought it was necessary to take eight lives along the way. Those are costs that are too expensive for any branch of the military to pay just to cover up some lapse in judgement or failure to complete one's mission."

"So, let me get this straight in my mind. You are beginning with the theory that espionage, or something to that effect, was involved in this crash and we need to find out what that something was?"

"I'm not totally convinced that is the case, but I'm keeping my mind open to that possibility."

"Why?"

"First, one of those C5 Super Galaxy aircraft don't just crash. They have auto pilots, all types of sensory equipment to indicate stalls and elevation correction—technical things that would prevent a simple crash that has been indicated from what we know so far. In fact, the tower covering the flight could have talked one of the airmen aboard into possibly landing the aircraft after the deaths of the pilots, assuming they died before the actual crash."

"And you're thinking maybe the collusion went beyond the cockpit of the C5, and that the tower and ground crew may have been complicit in the crash?"

"I'm trying to add up all the reasons a bird like that would be allowed to crash without herculean efforts being made to prevent such a tragedy, and I don't see those efforts having been made. That's one thing I will be looking for. I want to talk to the air traffic controllers, the mechanical crew that prepared the C5 for the flight, and I want to particularly examine the black boxes retrieved from the crash site to try and put a logical scenario together defining the crash. Right now, I don't buy suicide or accidental poisoning, or whatever the OAFME is selling!"

"It sounds like we have quite a job ahead of us, Colonel," Claire said. "By the way, you do look dashing in your military uniform!"

"Oh, hush!"

As they approached the hangar area of the base, they saw that an extremely high, chain-link fence had been erected to cordon off the hangars from the remaining area of the tarmac of the airport. There were two jeeps, two soldiers with automatic weapons guarding the entrance into the largest hangar, and they were being stopped by these soldiers for questioning. These were not airmen—these were U.S. Marines, fully armed and looking seasoned and dangerous. The lead soldier saluted the Colonel, asked him his business, and inspected his papers.

"Please state your specific reason for wanting to enter this facility, Colonel."

"My orders are clear and specific, Gunny. I suggest you allow us entry immediately, unless you would like to explain why you are detaining representatives of the Chief of Staff for the U.S.A.F. at the Pentagon. I can make that call if you prefer." The Marine gunnery sergeant looked at the papers once more, motioned for the other guard to unlock and open the gates, and he waved Butch and Claire into the restricted area. He saluted once more as he returned to his post.

"That was interesting. I guess we're home free now," Claire said.

"Don't bet on it. There will be C.I.D., or Special Ops people, in the hangar, and we will have to do the same dance again once we are within spitting distance of that C5 wreckage." Almost as if Butch had been a soothsayer, as they pulled up to the outside of the hangar that held the debris of Flight C5-SGM12 they were met again with men bearing automatic weapons. However, this time the military men appeared to be U.S. Navy Seals. The routine was much the same as when they were accosted earlier, with the exception that they were asked to leave their vehicle, permit to a pat down search, and a short walk through a magnetometer.

"My partner and I are authorized to carry concealed firearms, and before we part with them, I will need to speak to the commander of the Joint Base Charleston," Butch said. He showed the navy guard his papers, and after a short call to somewhere else on the base, they were permitted to keep their weapons and to enter the hangar.

"Wow! Look at that wreckage!" Claire said. She was observing a gigantic area of the hangar, systematically marked off with yellow crime tape, with various parts of the ruined fuselage placed strategically in various areas. "It's quite a reality to know what happens to aluminum when it comes in contact with an immovable surface at hundreds of miles an hour." She looked off to the right of the main wreckage and observed what was remaining of the wings of the giant aircraft. One of the wings was scorched almost beyond recognition, indicating that the wing tank must have ruptured when it crashed to the ground. The other wing was pretty much intact, with the exception that it had been broken into two large pieces.

"Let's see if the cockpit and instrument panel survived the crash," Butch said. They walked carefully to the area where the pilot and copilot had been sitting, and Butch was surprised to see that nothing of the flight deck was remaining in the debris. Butch indicated to a guard and motioned him over to them.

"What happened to the cockpit instrument panel and the controls of the aircraft?"

"I'm just a guard, Colonel. You'll have to ask those questions to someone above my rank."

"And the black boxes?"

"They are not here, Sir. My answer would be the same as to the previous question." Butch was getting very pissed, and he approached the guard who appeared to be the ranking serviceman in the detail.

"Who is the commander of this base?"

"Sir? I'm not sure I know what you're asking."

"What I want to know is who is the general or admiral that has the ultimate authority at this base. It's a simple question."

"I guess that would be General Leonard Lockhart, Sir."

"I need someone to get him on the phone for me—now!"

"Yes, sir. I will try, but I can't promise he is available."

"Just tell his gatekeeper that I am on direct orders from the U.S.A.F. Chief of Staff from the Pentagon. If he needs me to come to see him in person, that's fine as well. But either I see him, or I will bring a ton of trouble down on this base like it has never seen!"

"Yes, Sir. Let me see what I can do." The guard excused himself for a few minutes while he made a call to his superiors, and they called theirs, and so forth. In a matter of minutes, the phone was handed to Butch. He answered and asked who he was talking to.

"This is Colonel Fred Sweeney. I'm assuming that I am speaking to Colonel Butch Todd?" the question came back.

"That is correct, Colonel. I am on a special mission, originated and backed by General Brown of the U.S.A.F., and I have letters of authorization with me to prove my claim. The impression I have been given since I have arrived here is that someone at this base has something to hide. The last thing I want to do is have General Tecumseh Brown get directly involved in this investigation, but I am not beyond reaching out to his office if I am continually stalled in my investigation. Do you understand, Colonel?" There was silence for a minute, and then the line seemed to change, and Butch heard someone else pick up the telephone.

"This is General Lockhart. Who am I speaking with?" The senior commander seemed to be miffed that he had to deal with this investigator personally. Butch decided that now was the time to strike—while the coals were hot!

"General, my name is Colonel Butch Todd. It was my understanding that the Office of the Joint Chiefs of Staff at the Pentagon would have contacted your office about my investigation regarding Flight C5-SGM12. I would assume you would only be informed and not a person of contact, but I am finding irregularities that I do not wish to report back to the Pentagon about without some clarification from you or your staff." Butch asked the last question and shut up. He knew that he could not enact more pressure than silence upon the general once Butch had made his dramatic statement. Butch also knew that a general didn't reach flag rank without dodging a few land mines and other impediments along the way.

"Colonel, of course my office is willing to aid your research as much as is feasibly possible. Can you tell me exactly what you need to pursue your orders from General Brown?"

"Yes, Sir. I will be happy to share that information with you. I need to have access to all, not just a part, but *all* of the wreckage of Flight C5-SGM12, the cockpit and instruments that survived the crash, as well as the black boxes that were retrieved after the crash. Anything less than those items will constitute my having to contact the Pentagon for assistance in securing them."

"We will help you, Colonel, but you best remember that you are on *my* base, operating at *my* pleasure, and you will need to obey *my* rules during your investigation. I want to hear you acknowledge that I informed you and that you are cognizant of those facts." Butch could see the bluster of the general through the telephone lines!

"General, I acknowledge what you have said, and I will be willing to work within the guidelines of your office, but I should also inform you that my authority goes beyond the Pentagon, if you understand what I mean?" There was silence on the line, then the line went dead.

"How did that go?" Claire asked Butch once he had hung up from speaking to General Lockhart.

"Not too well, but not too bad, either." Butch handed the telephone back to the guard and made his next request.

"Please call whoever you need to for us to be ushered into the area where the wreckage of the cockpit, the flight deck, and the black box recorders are being held." The guard nodded, stepped away once more for a few minutes, and indicated for Butch and Claire to get into the jeep that was sitting in front of the hangar.

"I will take you there, Colonel," the young guard said, and they were off and heading for a distant hangar within another secure compound. No stops were needed this time, and the jeep wheeled into the hangar and stopped. Butch and Claire got out of the jeep, the driver spoke briefly to the guard on duty, and they were shown into a much smaller area that had several smaller zippered tents populating the floor area.

"The only restrictions you have, Colonel, is that you are not to remove any material of any kind from this hangar. You may study, photo, document, and interpret anything you find worthy of your time, but nothing can be removed," was the command from a tough-looking Marine sergeant who was holding an HK 416 - 5.56 carbine, fully loaded and strapped against his chest with a camo sling.

"Sergeant Thomas, I will need someone to set up a copier, facsimile line, and a dedicated and secure telephone line directly connected to the Pentagon. Can you get that done?"

"Absolutely, Colonel. It may take us a few hours to get those things done, but we should have completed your request by ten-hundred hours tomorrow morning. I will notify the guards that you and your assistant inspector are allowed back into this hangar. You shouldn't have too much trouble getting back in tomorrow morning. If anyone tries to detain you, tell them SGT Baygents authorized your entrance. They can call me and verify any questions they may have. The Marine saluted Butch turned on his heel and disappeared into an unmarked door inside the hangar.

"It looks like you have been finally admitted to the 'Good Old Boys Club' at the Joint Base Charleston, Butch," Claire joked. "You know what I am beginning to think?"

"What?"

"If there's really nothing much to see here, they are going to a lot of trouble trying to prevent anyone from seeing it."

"In other words, if there is a lot of smoke, there must be fire somewhere?"

"Exactly. And they gave you this much trouble knowing you are a direct emissary from the Pentagon. Something tells me that there may be a good reason to look at Joint Base Charleston closely for possible involvement in anything irregular that can be found about Flight C5-SGM12."

"Maybe. I'm glad you have my back. I'm also glad you are a very suspicious person!" Butch smiled at Claire, and she returned the expression.

"Let's go back to town, create a checklist to cover when we get back into the hangar tomorrow morning, and plan for a nice dinner at Anson's on Market Street."

"I really enjoyed 82 Queen for lunch. Is Anson's as good for dinner as 82 Queen was for lunch?"

"Oh, yeah. Just let me order for you and you will not be disappointed."

"As long as you're paying!"

"Me, and Uncle Sam!"

* * *

Butch and Claire drove back to the Battery, they went to their respective rooms, changed their clothes into something less formal, and met on the patio just outside the registration desk area. While it felt like fall in Ashburn when Butch and Claire left the Cullman County area of Alabama, South Carolina falls were not quite the same as those in most other Southern cities. First, the humidity persisted in Charleston until late fall, and sometimes until winter, so shorts and polo shirts were the common attire of out-of-town visitors to the Holy City until frost, which might not come until sometime in December.

"Why is Charleston referred to as the 'Holy City?' I thought that Rome, Italy, was considered the Holy City?" Claire asked.

"It's a long story. Are you sure you want to know?"

"Of course, or I wouldn't have asked you."

"I'll give you the short answer. According to legend, when visitors began to come to Charleston in the late 1600s and early 1700s, there were numerous churches and cathedrals being constructed all over the city—religious Protestant denominations, as well as Judaism and Roman Catholicism orders immigrants had brought with them. For this reason, Charleston earned the nickname of "Holy City" as it was known for its tolerance for all religions and it numerous historic churches."

"So, what are we going to do this afternoon? It's only 2:00 PM and we have four or five hours before dinner. What does one do in Charleston when not eating in one of its fine restaurants?"

"Let's go for a stroll down Meeting Street to the Battery. It's a nice day for a walk."

"What is the Battery? It sounds like a place where they manufacture batteries for various things."

"Oh, no. It's nothing like that. The Battery is a landmark defensive seawall and promenade in Charleston, and it was named for a civil-war coastal defense artillery battery at the site. Cannons faced Charleston Harbor during the American Revolution, and again in the Civil War, and they were placed on the Battery grounds to protect the City of Charleston from attack by the British forces in the American Revolution, and then against the Yankees in the Civil War. There are many cannons still in place on the Battery just like they were 150 years ago."

"Are we dressed appropriately for such a walk?" Claire had on shorts and a blouse, and Butch was wearing shorts and a tank top. "I feel somewhat casual in my current attire."

"Except for dinner restaurants, plays at the Dock Street Theatre, and other formal invitations in Charleston, everyone is pretty casual most of the time. With the humidity at 80+% most of the time, one needs to dress coolly if one is going to be walking the streets of Charleston."

"Then let's go," Claire said cheerily. "I'm ready to be indoctrinated into Charleston culture."

"That may take a while, but I'll work on it." Butch smiled at his pretty assistant and motioned her toward the gate to the patio by the Gaslight Inn. They walked through the Charleston Market, one of the oldest outdoor markets of its kind in America. It was built in 1831, and contrary to rumors, slaves were not sold at this market. They were sold, however, just down the street at the corner of Broad and East Bay Streets, further down the peninsula toward the Battery and the Four Corners of Law."

"The Four Corners of Law?"

"The intersection of Meeting Street and Broad Street was commonly referred to as the Four Corners of Law, because all four levels of public government was represented on one of the corners there: the U.S. Post Office (Federal); Charleston City Hall (City); County Courthouse (State Law); and St. Michael's Episcopal Church (God's law.) What was possibly more interesting is who first referred to that intersection as the Four Corners of Law. It was none other than Robert Ripley, founder of *Believe it or Not.* He made that observation in 1930, almost 100 years earlier, and his naming of the corner stuck."

"If you're not pulling my leg, Charleston has more history about its historical area than anyplace I know."

"You have no idea!"

Butch and Claire walked the historic streets of the Battery area of Charleston, up and down Tradd Street, Legare Street, Lenwood Blvd, Gibbes Street, and King Street. King Street had become the shopping district of the Historical District many years ago, and it was the only street in downtown Charleston with more restaurants, retail stores, and garages than historic homes. They stopped in a park which was located behind the welcome center for the city, had a cold iced tea from a street vendor, and rested before they headed back up Meeting Street to the Gaslight Inn. As they entered the Inn from the private patio entrance off Meeting street, Butch suggested that they rest their muscles by enjoying a brief dip in the Jacuzzi located just off their rooms. Claire agreed, and they went into their rooms to change into proper attire for swimming. Butch had gotten into the Jacuzzi before Claire had returned from putting on her suit, and he admired the hard, firm body his assistant displayed in her skimpy two-piece bathing suit. As Claire eased into the 106-degree water she sighed.

"Wow! That's warm. Is this supposed to cool me off?"

"The way an outside Jacuzzi works is for the warm water to open your pores, and as you cool off the evaporation from the moisture on your skin makes you feel much cooler."

"If you say so." However, the longer she sat in the Jacuzzi, the more comfortable she became. "Let's just stay in here until dinnertime, have dinner delivered, and take a nap on one of our rooms."

"One cannot do that sort of thing in Charleston, Claire. Dinner is an adventure, and it must be experienced first-hand. We can get out in twenty or thirty minutes, get a quick shower, and relax on the patio by the registration desk until dinnertime. Allen told me that he had a celloist coming at 4:30 PM to serenade the guests for about an hour. I think our reservations are for 6:00 PM, and it's only a short walk to Anson's from here."

"Now I can understand why you wanted to stay here, instead of a Marriott or other major chain hotel. The hotel is lovely, and the entire experience will be memorable when we have returned to Ashburn."

"That's the plan. When you finish getting ready for dinner, bring your portfolio and a pen with you to the patio. We can begin making our grand plan for tomorrow's workday before we get too tired and ready for bed."

"You do realize that someone could be observing us as we sit in the Jacuzzi, take walks down to the Battery, and take our meals in fancy restaurants. They may even be observing whether or not we disappear into each other's rooms before bedtime. Have you considered those possibilities?"

"I have. First, we are both adults of a consenting age; second, you are not a military person, so I can fraternize with you without endangering our mission; and third, I don't care what people think of me when it comes to my personal life. Until someone changes the U.S. Constitution, I will enjoy my red-blooded American freedoms how and when I desire!"

"Ok. That's just fine with me. I have no qualms about being with you in public or private. I guess that puts to rest any concerns we might have between us."

* * *

When Claire reached the patio, she observed Butch enjoying the accompaniment of a young man playing a cello, and he was dressed in a black tuxedo, white tie, and shiny black dress shoes. She wondered how anyone could sit outside in the humidity of Charleston, S.C., in any kind of a suit and not simply melt into the brick pavers. Somehow, this young man seemed not to be bothered by the heat, humidity, or anything else around him. He made that cello sing as sweetly as Claire had ever heard anyone play such an instrument. And that was saying something since she had been playing classical music on the road for over ten years prior to joining up with Butch in Ashburn.

"Bach, 6th Cello Suite," Claire announced quietly as she took a chair beside Butch on the patio. Butch had commandeered an open carafe of white wine and two glasses, and he had poured a glass for both he and Claire to sip and enjoy the music. The young celloist nodded pleasantly to Claire, acknowledging her knowledge of the piece he was playing, and he continued on totally lost in his performance. When he had finished playing everyone in the sitting area of the patio gave the celloist a nice applause. He grinned, picked up his bow, and began a Brittan piece.

"I see that you recognized the Bach piece our celloist was playing. That should not surprise me, especially since you played on the worldwide circuit for many years. I like Bach, but it all sounds the same to me. I couldn't recognize one of his pieces from another if my life depended on it!"

"That's because you were flying jet planes at twice the speed of sound while I was learning to distinguish one Bach piece from another. We simply have different talents, Butch. I can live with that." Claire smiled warmly at Butch, and he returned her smile.

"It's 5:45 PM, and our dinner reservations are at 6:00 PM. Anson's will hold a table reservation for only ten minutes before allowing someone to take the spot. Are you ready for dinner?"

"Absolutely. Do we need a taxi to get to Anson's in fifteen minutes?"

"No. It's actually just a couple of blocks due east of here on Market Street. We can 'window shop' along the way." They rose, Butch put a ten-dollar bill in the celloist's empty wine glass that had been placed nearby on a table for just such a tip, and they walked casually out into the heat of a typical Charleston early evening. When the sun set over the peninsula that held the City of Charleston in its grip, the offshore breezes would cool the city down considerably, and that would make their walk back from Anson's more pleasant than the walk over. They arrived at Anson's with five minutes to spare, and they were immediately seated in a quaint nook that overlooked Church Street and the bustling area of the horse-drawn carriages. The only negative that could be attributed to eating at Anson's was the occasional odor that wafted down the street from the corner of Pinckney and Market, the location where the horse-drawn carriages originated and where the horses were fed and stabled. It was difficult to find anything objectionable about Anson's in any way. Butch had ordered the crispy flounder with local seasonal vegetables, a bottle of white wine, and a dessert known only as 'Death by Chocolate,' to round off their meal. As they walked back through the Market on their way to the Gaslight Inn, Claire seemed totally at ease with her place in this this historic city.

"I ate enough for two people. Geez! I won't be able to fit into my clothes if I keep eating this way while we are in Charleston. By the way, what style of cooking would you say that most Charlestonian employ?"

"Oh, that's easy. It's commonly referred to as Lowcountry cuisine. It is absolutely traditionally accepted as the official cuisine associated with South Carolina Lowcountry and the Georgia coast."

"I don't think I've ever heard the term 'Lowcountry.' Where did that term originate and what does it represent?"

"According to Wikipedia," the Lowcountry (sometimes Low Country or just low country) is a geographic and cultural region along South Carolina's coast, including the Sea Islands. What it really means is the area of South Carolina below the Fall Line—the Sandhills (the ancient seacoast) which run the width of the state from Aiken County to Chesterfield County. The area above the Sandhills was known as the Up Country and the area below was known as the Low Country."

"Well, aren't you little Mr. Encyclopedia?" Claire said as they walked slowly toward Meeting Street. "How do you know so much about this area?"

"This was my R&R destination as many times as possible when I was on active duty with the U.S.A.F. I would come to Charleston, check into the Gaslight Inn, and roam the streets for two weeks getting to know every crack and cranny of the city, eat in a different restaurant every meal, and go back to my duty location fully relaxed and intoxicated with Lowcountry living."

"It almost sounds like it was a religious experience for you."

"It was. I could live in one of the Bachelor houses here and never drive my car again. There is really nothing outside the Battery area of Charleston that I would need to search for. It is a self-contained thriving market area."

"So, why didn't you retire to Charleston, instead of Ashburn? You were 'footloose and fancy free,' weren't you when you came back to Ashburn for a visit?"

"I came back for the funeral of a great teacher and a fine man, as you know. Things just happened that held my attention long enough to divert me from moving here to Charleston. I might still move here one day."

"I think it is a lovely place, steeped in history, and every bit as charming as you described it to me before we arrived. Thank you for exposing me to it." Claire stopped, reached up to Butch, and gave him a simple kiss on his lips.

"What was that for?"

“Why does there always have to be a reason for you men to express emotions? You guys are all Neanderthals!” Claire continued to walk toward the Gaslight Inn while Butch tried to figure out how he had upset her. He was glad that he didn’t have to watch everything he said, every minute of every day, like he figured would be the case if her were married to a sensitive woman like Claire. Why couldn’t a guy just say what was on his mind without be reamed over the coals? Women! He would never understand them.

When they arrived back at the Gaslight Inn, Claire complained of a headache, and begged off sharing the Jacuzzi with Butch. He said he understood, donned his bathing suit, and sat in the warm, bubbly water for half an hour. Afterward, the showered, got into the elevated, queen-sized canopy bed, and slept the sleep of the dead.

Chapter 8

Deception

No one liked having "the wool pulled over their eyes," and Butch especially resented anyone attempting to hide important facts about the crash of Flight C5-SGM12 from him. He already had a chip on his shoulder from the running around that he had gotten the day before, so Butch came armed with defiance to the hangar at Joint Base Charleston the next morning. When he saw SGT Thomas, he immediately made his demands in no uncertain terms.

"Sergeant, I'm going to say this one time to you today, and if my requests are stymied or delayed for any reason, I'm going to hold you personally responsible. What that will entail is a possible Article 32 being issued against you. (Article 32 of the Uniform Code of Military Justice (UCMJ) requires an independent investigation of all charges and specifications against an accused prior to a general court-martial (GCM). The accusation alone could prevent a career military person from promotion consideration due to the black mark left in that soldier's military jacket.)

"Colonel, I'm just trying to do my job and follow the orders I have been given by my commanding officer. If you disagree with any action I take today, please inform me and I will put you in touch with my C.O. The two of you can work out the details, Sir. I have to obey my orders, as you know, to the best of my ability, without question or hesitation."

"If your C.O. gave you an order to shoot me or my assistant, would you blindly follow that order as well?" Butch asked. He was getting very mad as the questioning continued.

"I have not been given such an order, Colonel." Sergeant Thomas answered the question the only way he knew how to answer. He was straightforward and honest, though tactless and frank.

"I want to see the control panel and the flight deck of Flight C5-SGM12. Is that available?"

"Yes, Sir. Please follow me." SGT Thomas led Butch and Claire down a long corridor, guarded by two Marines in camo uniforms, standing at attention with automatic weapons at the ready position. They entered a room which was more akin to an operating room than that of a warehouse storage facility. The large flight deck of the giant plane had been removed, pieced back together as well as possible, and a catwalk with various landings had been constructed around it, giving any observer access to all parts of the equipment, dials, and levers that seemed to be everywhere. Butch dismissed SGT Thomas, and when the door closed, he just looked in amazement at the sheer volume of mechanical hardware that made up the flight deck.

"Have you ever seen anything like this, Claire?"

"Good grief! I would need a schematic to just decide where to search for a problem. How can one pilot handle all the gauges, switches, and devices that I am looking at? There must be over 100 switches alone."

"This is the cockpit of one of the largest aircrafts in the world. One pilot *never* has complete control of the flight deck of a military C5 aircraft. There are always two pilots, and sometimes three—the Flight Engineer. Each pilot has a checklist of things he or she is to do before the flight takes off or lands. Only when the flight is actually in the air does the pilot have complete control of the aircraft, and he can be relieved at any time by the co-pilot or the flight engineer if needed. That's what makes the initial diagnosis of *'death by suicide'* difficult for me to believe. There are so many opportunities for a crew to take over the flight deck, in case the pilot is unstable or if he falls ill during the flight, and according to the official report we have been given the co-pilot and the flight engineer seemed to sit by and let the pilot fly a $238 million dollar aircraft with eight souls aboard into the ground. That doesn't add up for a commercial flight, and it definitely doesn't sound credible for a military flight."

"What are we looking for to give us an indication that what you are assuming is true?"

"A struggle between the pilots, or some non-life-threatening injury found on the copilot or flight engineer's body that may have occurred prior to the crash. That's why we need to see the autopsies of all of the crew, listen to the recordings in the Black Boxes, and inspect this flight deck thoroughly. We are trying to make chicken soup without the chicken!"

"You lost me there, Butch. What does chicken soup have to do with all of this?" Butch smiled at Claire's question. He had forgotten many of the silly sayings his folks had expressed over the years, but the one about chicken soup was one of his favorites.

"Just something my mom and grandmother used to say. However, they were correct in assuming that you couldn't make scrambled eggs without eggs, or chicken soup without a chicken! In other words, common sense should enter the equations somewhere, and I don't see that it has been used here so far."

"Assuming we find something amiss with the arrangement between the pilots and the crew, how does that help us with POTUS and his supposition that espionage was a possible motive in the crash? One would think that POTUS and the Chief of Staff may be hiding some information that they believe is too sensitive to make available to us and that might be compromised during our investigation. Something is not adding up for me from our source."

"I know, that crossed my mind as well. We can't worry about 'what-ifs' right now. We need to deduct the truth from the facts that we can determine exists and let the chips fall where they may."

"Since we are supposed to report *only* to General Brown, where's the harm in telling us all the government knows? That logic baffles me."

"Take it from one who has dealt with the U.S. Government for years when I tell you that they trust no one—not even themselves at times!"

"Like you said. We investigate and make our report. That's all we were hired to do. Right?"

"Right," Butch said, but Claire could see in his response that he would not simply stop at that if he thought there was more to learn. This was going to be an exciting ride! She had to put those thoughts out of her mind as they searched the flight deck for clues.

"What are we looking for, Butch? I may be looking at exactly what we need to know but not know what that is. It's very frustrating."

"Let me look at the controls and dials. What I want you to do is look in the specific space that each pilot sat during the flight. It appears that the engineers have reconstructed the flight deck to pretty much what it was before the crash. If they did what they were supposed to do, they would have used forensics to determine where everything and everyone was prior to the crash, and they would have tried to reconstruct things that way. In particular, check the seat belt configurations, the life rafts under each seat—things like that. We never know which missing piece of evidence will lead to something more important and specific in our search for the truth."

Butch took out his small black detective's notebook and made notes about each gauge, lever, and switch that he examined. When he had finished with that task, he took a legal sized notebook page and sketched the exact gauges as they were visible to him during his investigation. Claire continued to search around the seats and spaces where the pilots hat sat and performed their routine chores during the flight. It took over an hour, but eventually both detectives believed that they had gleaned as much forensics information as was possible to recover from the flight deck. Butch saw that Claire had finished her job and was sitting quietly in the flight engineer's jump seat waiting for Butch to finish as well.

"That just about does it for me. Did you get to check out everything around the pilot's space? Did you see anything that might indicate foul play from anyone in the cockpit?"

"I think it might be best If we waited until we returned to the Gaslight Inn to ponder our results. Nothing jumped out and screamed sabotage, but there may have been some abnormalities that I discovered. Where do we go from here?"

"The Black Boxes," Butch said. "We simply must have access to them or nothing else we find will matter." Butch indicated to SGT Thomas that he was ready to be taken to the location where the Black Boxes were being stored. They boarded a Hummer, the sergeant wheeled the vehicle around ninety degrees, and they sped off toward another small hangar close by. Once they entered the hangar, the sergeant disappeared back outside. Butch immediately spotted the orange, shoe-box sized metal boxes and headed that way.

"These are not black, Butch. They are bright orange," Claire said as she remarked on the physical characteristics of the boxes that held both the flight data recordings as well as the cockpit voice recorder. He smiled a knowing smile at her before he explained the nomenclature of the recording devices.

"They are painted fluorescent orange so they can be more easily detected in debris at a crash site. While they were developed originally in Australia in the 1950s to help detect why an aircraft went down, they were originally encased in a hardened steel case and simply painted black. Hence, they got the name Black Boxes. Over the years, it was determined that by painting them bright orange made it easier for these boxes to be located after a crash, so now all Black Boxes are painted orange. It's an industry standard."

"What happens if the aircraft crashes into the sea or swamp? How do they find the Black Boxes in those incidences?"

"Good question, Claire. Most aircraft today have an underwater location beacon that beeps consistently for up to 30 days while the rescue and recovery teams are trying to locate the crash and the Black Boxes."

"I had General Brown's aide supply us with a special MP3 player so we can listen to the recordings of Flight C5-SGM12. Bear with me for a moment while I transfer the data from the recorder to the player, and then we can listen to it together." Butch seemed to fumble with the gadget that he had been supplied with to listen to the recordings, and in just a few minutes he had them keyed up and ready to play. Everything was routine on the cockpit voice recorder (CVR) until three minutes before the flight data recording (FDR) registered an all systems failure. After the last FDR recording there was nothing but silence.

"Play the CVR recording once more and turn the volume up as loud as you can so we can try and understand what was being said in the last minutes of the flight," Claire said. Butch rewound the tapes, keyed the CVR recording back up to the last three or four minutes of the tape, and they listened again for anything out of the ordinary that they had not recognized the first time.

"I feel really bad, Buddy," the voice of Colonel McGee could be heard over the whine of the engines which appeared to be laboring against some outside force.

"I don't feel so good myself, Colonel. Do you think it was something we ate? Where is Captain Allgood? He should be on the bridge here with us. Call him over your radio and tell him to report to the cockpit immediately. We have a serious problem that I cannot seem to focus enough on to fix," the Colonel said.

No voice recording of the page of Captain Marshall Allgood, the flight engineer for Flight C5-SGM12, was heard over the CVR. Butch calculated that the poison that Major Buddy Hawkins had consumed somehow had completed its work and he was probably dead.

"Mayday, mayday," the colonel spoke briefly into the CVR, but after that request he also went silent. A minute later a very loud crashing sound was heard on the CVR, and then there were multiple explosions that lasted about two minutes. Butch calculated that if the doomed flight had been doing practice takeoffs and landings, one of the activities that pilots of warbirds performed on a routine basis, that the fuel tanks were probably topped off at Joint Base Charleston before the training flight began. The wreckage of the fuselage confirmed to Butch that the wing tanks had probably ruptured when the aircraft hit the ground at a high speed, possibly allowing the Jet-A fuel catch fire. While the jet fuel is not as flammable as many would

believe, if it is being atomized when an aircraft crashes it will ignite and cause the fuselage and anything it touches to burst into flames. That's why many jet crashes allow people who have not been killed upon impact to be rescued and helped safely off the plane. If the fuel was not being atomized, something that a forensics investigator could discover is directed to search for such a thing, then there most likely was something else aboard to ignite it—like a bomb. Butch explained the differences between Jet-A fuel, diesel, kerosene, heating oil, and gasoline to Claire. She understood the concept of atomizing fuel into a fine mist so it could be burned, so Butch didn't have to go into a remedial and drawn-out description of why the Jet-A fuel probably was ignited by something other than the crash of Flight C5-SGM12 alone.

"Did you read the summation of the NTSB report on the cause of the crash verses what we think may have happened?"

"I did, and I was extremely disappointed that nowhere in the multiple pages of reporting was there any theory that the crash could have been caused by a planted incendiary or other explosive device."

"Why do you think that happened? It's almost as if they were not looking objectively relating to why the crash occurred. What might make them overlook something so basic as possible sabotage?"

"If you remember when we first discussed the details of the crash of C5-SGM12 with Colonel Summers, he told us immediately that Colonel McGee had been suspected of possible suicide by aircraft, and it was just assumed that the NTSB and every other investigating crew would find that to be the case."

"I don't remember anything about a note from the colonel stating that he was going to kill himself, do you?"

"Not only was there no note, when one listens to the CVR, it is pretty obvious that neither Colonel McGee nor Major Hawkins knew that they had been poisoned. They were fine, until they *were not fine*, according to the voice recording we just heard. To my ears, they appeared to be thinking that they had ingested something in their last meal that might have given them food poisoning. Isn't that what you heard?"

"It is, and I will tell you something else I heard that I'm sure you heard as well. Captain Marshall Allgood had disappeared from the flight deck. According to my limited knowledge of a C5 flight deck, it is on the same order as a Boeing 747. Right?"

"With some modifications, but basically—yes."

"I think what we need to be investigating is an accurate accounting of the bodies recovered, or parts of bodies, from the crash. According to the initial report there were three pilots and five crewmen. Right?"

"I think your numbers are correct."

"As a layperson, and not a jet fighter pilot," Claire smiled at Butch as she clarified her limited knowledge of all things avionics, "I would want to know how difficult it would have been for Captain Marshall Allgood to leave the plane during its training exercises without causing any suspicion?"

Butch thought for a moment, took out his yellow lined notebook, and started making some calculations. After a few moments, Butch looked up at Claire and looked astonished.

"I am beginning to believe that the S.O.B. got off the plane somehow before it crashed. It is highly likely that either the recovery of bodies is an incorrect count, or an additional body was placed on the aircraft to insure it would be counted as one of the servicemen once the investigation began to account for those on board. Stall speed on a jet that large is probably somewhere around 100 knots, or 115 MPH, and that would be landing or taking off. It is possible that Captain Allgood could have left the C5A by way of a drag chute or some other equipment to slow down his departure from the plane momentarily so he would not be severely injured when he made contact with the ground."

"How would that work?"

"I'm not sure that it would work, but if I were to guess, I would say that a sled type of escape capsule, aided by a drag chute, might make it possible."

"Wouldn't someone on the aircraft notice something like that going on?"

"Not necessarily. You see, when a cargo plane the size of a C5A comes in for a landing when practicing touch and go exercises, something as small as a chute or sled could easily be lost in the moment."

"Where would the chute and sled be hidden for him to pull something like that off?"

"C5A aircraft have the same landing gear mechanism as the Boeing 747—four separate wheel wells, with 28 aircraft tires filling those spaces. A trained escape artist could place a sled strategically into one of the rear wheel wells and launch himself out of the bay when the C5A begins to lift off from the runway."

"That would be pretty dangerous, wouldn't it?"

"Not as dangerous as taking your chances of living through a crash of the aircraft when it falls out of the sky flying hundreds of miles an hour."

"And you think that Captain Allgood may have poisoned the pilot and the copilot before exiting the plane? Is that your theory?"

"Do you have a better one?"

"Nope. As ridiculous as your supposition appears, it does seem possible. But how would Captain Allgood get away quickly enough without being observed if the C5A were circling the airport practicing 'touch and goes' for more than one time?"

"I don't know everything about espionage and sabotage, but I imagine Captain Allgood had at least one accomplice, or maybe more than one. They may have had a getaway truck or car disguised as an official vehicle. Who is going to question a U.S.A.F. vehicle with all the proper markings driving around on the tarmac? Nobody!"

"Where do we begin discrediting an official U.S. Government report that found nothing of the sort of things we are suggesting at the scene of the crash? Can we get the autopsy reports on all eight bodies recovered or identified that were reportedly on Flight C5-SGM12? If so, those records should either identify the remains of Captain Allgood, or there will be no evidence of his presence on that flight when it came crashing to the ground."

"What will that tell us?"

"Butch, there may have been nine people on that flight, but only eight reported to be there. The only other way there could be eight bodies, and one of them not being Captain Allgood, would be if a body were placed on the aircraft in anticipation of the crash and the knowledge that there would be a forensics investigation after the tragedy. Do you have a better solution?"

"I agree with you. The most plausible deduction, and it's hardly believable, of the crash was specific poisoning of the pilot and copilot, with the flight engineer somehow exiting the aircraft before it crashed. How we will get General Brown and POTUS to believe such a theory may be a bit more difficult!"

"Just remember what Sherlock Holmes said: '*When you have eliminated the impossible, whatever remains, however improbable, must be the truth?'*

"And you're hoping POTUS is a Sherlock Holmes fan?" Butch couldn't help but laugh at his own supposition.

"I'm just hoping General Brown and POTUS are realists—facts don't lie."

"Let's continue our investigation as if we had not deduced the possibility of an escape from Flight C5-SGM12 and see where it takes us. Right now, I'd put even money on the fact that none of those bodies in the base morgue is that of Captain Allgood." Claire agreed and they continued to pour over all the evidence available to them in search of an alternative cause of the crash. They came up empty.

"I hope you have enjoyed your visit to Charleston, because we need to check out of the Gaslight Inn, get on a plane to the Pentagon, and bring General Brown up to date on what we have discovered and our deductions from that new evidence."

"No more trips to 82 Queen or Anson's," she whined.

"Tell you what I will agree on. Let's go to the hotel, have Allen Johnson get our bags ready for checkout, bring our car to the hotel from the parking lot, and we'll have one more lunch at 82 Queen before we leave."

"That's better than nothing. Too bad we can't just 'mail in' our report to the general and stay here another night or two. I never got to use the Jacuzzi."

"Opportunities wasted—sad memories of what could have been," Butch winked as he indicated to SGT Thomas to take them back to their car so they could check out of the base. In a matter of minutes, they were driving down I-26 toward the Battery and one last luncheon before they left for their meeting at the Pentagon.

"Shouldn't you call ahead?" Claire asked.

"I already did when we were leaving the base. The general will see us at 1600 hours."

"That's 4:00 PM in the afternoon?"

"Yes, that's how military time is expressed. It is used to prevent any mix-ups in whether the order was given at 4:00 AM or 4:00 PM."

"Very logical," Claire said. "Let's hope the same logic is applied to our final report on the crash of Flight C5-SGM12."

"We'll see," was all Butch had to say, but Claire knew he was thinking about how many other things could be considered once they had made their report to the Pentagon.

"Does this mean our mission has been accomplished and that we will be relieved of duty?"

"I cannot say at this point, but I rather doubt the U.S. Government will want to cease operations just because they discover who pulled the wool over their eyes."

"And why should they want us to continue once they have the facts?"

"Because, at that point they will be looking for a criminal who possibly sabotaged a major defense project, and then fled to avoid capture and interrogation. Who better to go after a criminal than two successful private detectives? Private detectives who have an unlimited amount of resources to get the job done?"

"I think I see your point." They pulled up to the Gaslight Inn, informed Allen of their immediate departure, and requested that within the next hour their car be brought to the Inn for them to depart the hotel and Charleston for a destination unspoken. Allen smiled, agreed to Butch's requests, and the two detectives walked down to 82 Queen for a parting lunch.

Chapter 9

Revelation

Standing before General Brown, Butch recited his planned delivery of the facts of their investigation with no interruptions by the general or Claire. When he had finished his debriefing, he sat down respectfully and took in a deep breath of air. He had not been aware of how tense he had become during his explanation of the investigation that he and Claire had performed in Charleston.

"Let me see if I have the facts straight in my mind," the general said. "You believe that there were nine, not eight, people aboard Flight C5-SGM12, that one of them poisoned both pilots, escaped through the wheel well space during touch-and-goes, and that that person is now at large in our country? Is that the gist of it?"

"Yes, Sir. That's pretty much all we have learned so far. As you can see from the supporting documentation, there was no positive identification of a Captain Allgood in the remains of the crash. In fact, I would not be surprised if 'Captain Allgood' was a plant by our enemies, and that you will not find a military personnel jacket on him at all. That last comment is just a guess, General. We haven't had the time to check out every detail of this potential traitor. We wanted to get this report to you as soon as possible. And, as unbelievable as it may seem, we do think that someone could have escaped the aircraft during those touch-and-go exercises." Butch said nothing more, waiting for the general to thank them and relieve them of duty. However, that was not going to happen.

"Colonel, you and your assistant have done an excellent job rooting out the facts of this case, and I believe every word of it. However, you are not finished in your task of helping us find and prosecute whoever caused the crash of that C5A. I do believe for you to continue as a military officer may only bring more suspicion upon your investigation than performing the same services as a civilian. Therefore, as of this moment, you are relieved of your command, retired as a full-bird colonel in the U.S.A.F., as promised, and the results of your investigation will be considered final and sealed."

"Thank you, Sir. We really need to get back to our actual jobs in Ashburn, Alabama, as soon as possible." Butch and Claire rose from their chairs, but the general did not move.

"Please sit back down, Butch," the general said. "As of this moment you are a civilian again, not beholding to me or any other military officer in the country. However, I have a proposal to make you and Ms. Cavendish." Butch and Claire sat back down and waited for the general to speak. The general seemed to ponder his next words, and Butch was getting impatient waiting on him.

"Was there something else, General?"

"Butch, there's always something else, but in answer to your specific situation this is a proposal I am making. You don't have to accept it, and your response will not be noted in your military file if you reject my offer."

"What might that be, General?"

"The DOD wants to hire you and Ms. Cavendish to continue to investigate this imposter, Captain Marshall Allgood. We want him brought to justice. We would prefer that he be brought in alive, but you would have the authority to capture or terminate him with prejudice. I will not be able to make that judgement, but we will trust that your actions will be performed in the highest professional manner. As long as you identify, pursue, capture or terminate him, the job will be considered successfully completed."

"That type of operation might get to be expensive, General," Butch said.

"Do you still have the credit card that was issued to you before you began this investigation?"

"I do. I was going to hand it back to you now."

"Keep it. Besides all expenses that you have being paid by the government, we are sending a one-time payment to yours and Ms. Cavendish's banks in the amount of $100,000. Once the mission is complete, and that would entail the capture or termination of the suspect, we will send another $100,000 as a final payment. The military personnel helping your mayor in Ashburn will continue until your mission is complete. How does that sound to you? A simple detective job, hired and paid for by the U.S. Government."

Butch looked at Claire, now his partner in all things detective work, and she just gave a little shrug of her shoulders. Butch looked back at the general and asked a very important question.

"Deniability?"

"Deniability for what? Being a detective? I thought that was what your mark and trade was, Butch. Why would you want to deny being a detective?" Butch thought about it for a very short period of time and nodded. They had just secured the most reliable and largest client they would ever have.

"Butch and Claire shook the general's hand, they were escorted out of the building as in past visits, they boarded a helicopter to take them to the airfield, and in a matter of two hours they were deplaning the G700 private jet at the 117th

Wing of the National Guard in Birmingham. As they got into Butch's truck and headed for Ashburn, Claire looked intensely at Butch, and she told him that she was proud to be his partner.

"You know, I would never have had an opportunity to get so close to a major investigation such as this without my association with you."

"So, you feel you owe me a favor?" Butch teased.

"Just as soon as we arrive at home."

* * *

Butch and Claire enjoyed a quiet night in their rental house near the campus of Ashburn University. They had had a very exciting week. First the trip to the Pentagon, then on Joint Base Charleston and the lovely Lowcountry city of Charleston, S.C., and finishing the week with a return visit to the Pentagon once more. As weeks went, this one was truly an unusual one. Sitting in the kitchen of their apartment, sipping on black coffee and eating a bagel, Claire was pondering where their investigation might lead them from here.

"When do you plan to tell Mayor Hannity about our new assignment?"

"It's not really a new assignment. It's the continuation of our current assignment which we haven't completed yet."

"You can mince words with me, but you'd better have a better story than that for the mayor, or we may both be searching for new jobs after we dispense with the U.S.A.F. and their current use of our time and talents."

"Did you have something in mind?"

"Yeah. I think you need to sell it to him like you mean it. We are continuing in our role as investigators for the U.S.A.F.

until we discover who has been a traitor to our country, and we are going to bring him in 'Dead or Alive," just like the old west posters used to advertise."

"First of all, this is not the old west, and second, we may find and apprehend him, or we may not be able to locate him."

"That doesn't sound as official as my statement."

"Your statement is faulty. There is no assurance that we will succeed."

"Butch, I'm telling you if you are not forceful with Mayor Hannity, we could be looking at pink slips before long. He has to believe that we believe in what we are doing. Otherwise, he can just hire anyone to issue parking tickets and run radar on a quiet Cullman County road."

"Trust me. I have this covered," he said. "I think we need to make an appearance in the mayor's office. How long until you can make yourself presentable for such a meeting?"

"Give me twenty minutes."

True to her word, Claire was dressed in a business suit, had her hair pulled up in a fashionable knot on her head, and she was as ready as she was ever going to be to face Mayor Hannity. Butch had dressed in slacks, a sportscoat, no tie, and brown tie up shoes. This was their normal attire, and the absence of the uniform was a relief for Butch. The weather was clean and dry, so they decided to walk to the police station, which was just a few blocks away from where they were renting. As they walked along, Butch wanted to vocalize what they might say to Mayor Hannity once they were sitting in his office. They both felt good about the dialogue that they had planned when they walked into the Ashburn Police Station. Recognized by the desk sergeant, Butch and Claire got a friendly welcome and were asked what they were doing back in town.

"Hey, Joe," Butch said to SGT Joe Green. "Where's Leon?" Leon Cumberland was the middle-aged sergeant who normally sat in the Desk Sergeant's position.

"He took a few days off. Things have been very quiet around here, and the mayor has been letting us catch up on our off-duty time. I put in for a week's vacation for next week, assuming nothing major breaks out between now and then."

"How are the two new men working out for the department?"

"Seem to be doing quite well."

"Is PFC Connally in the office?"

"Go on back. I think she's back there somewhere. I haven't seen her leave since I've been here." Burch and Claire opened the hallway door and walked toward the chief's office. They found Elene Connally sitting in the chief's chair, going over a stack of paperwork which Butch did not envy. She looked up as they walked into the office, and she stood uncomfortably knowing that the police chief was present in the room.

"Sorry I didn't hear you come in, Chief. Do you want your office back?"

"No, Elene. We're still on assignment for the U.S.A.F. We're just in plain clothes now instead of my having to wear a stuffy military uniform."

"I don't think anyone was expecting you back so soon," she said. "Have you told Mayor Hannity that you're back?"

"His office is our next stop. I wanted to speak to you first before I visited with the mayor. How are the two military men working out as security people?"

"Very well for the department. I think they may be putting a damper on some of the locals, but that's probably because they are breaking the law in some way. Crime has been nonexistent since the general population discovered our new temporary officers. I have to admit it, they are a little intimidating."

"Is the mayor happy with the work those two men are doing for the police department and the city?"

"He must. We haven't gotten a hostile phone call from the mayor's office since those two started. I truly think the mayor will be sad when you have to send them on their way back to wherever they came from."

"The good news is that they will be with you a few more days while we wrap up our investigation for the U.S.A.F. Do you know if the mayor is in his office today?"

"I guess. Would you like for me to call over and let him know you're on the way to see him?"

"No, I think we'll just drop in on him. You're doing a great job as acting chief, so keep up the good work until I return."

"Yes, Sir." Elene got back to her paperwork and Butch and Claire let themselves out the back door of the station, heading over to the Ashburn City Hall and Mayor Hannity's office. Nothing in downtown Ashburn was more than ten minutes from anything else, and they were walking into city hall in less than ten minutes.

"Do you really think that 'dropping in on the mayor' is a good idea? Shouldn't we have a plan before we tell him that we are still on the U.S.A.F. payroll?" Claire asked.

"No. I think the more we think about how we will approach the mayor the more tenuous our situation will be. We simply need to tell him the truth and let the chips fall where they may. We didn't ask for this mission, but we need to finish it since we have agreed to begin it. I don't like walking away from any challenge."

"You, Sir, are honorable. I agree with you, but the mayor may tell us to take our U.S.A.F. job and not let the door hit us in the butt as we leave his office. Have you thought about that possibility?"

"Yep. I guess we just do what we think is right and live with the results. You are free to go back to work for the city. Who know, they may make you the Chief of Police!" He winked at her when he made the last statement.

"Ha, ha! You know that there's no way I'm going to abandon you or the mission at this point. I think there's more to this than the crashing of a $238 million dollar aircraft. That's what we need to investigate, in my opinion."

"From the mouth of babes," Butch said. They had reached city hall and the decision to either enter or not enter was immediately before them. Without hesitation, Butch pushed the door open, held it for Claire, and entered behind her into the lobby of the city municipal building. The receptionist saw them enter, spoke into the intercom on her desk, and welcomed them back to Ashburn.

"I hope you were successful in your mission for the government. Are you back for good?"

"Not exactly," Butch answered. The mayor walked into the lobby and indicated that he wanted Claire and Butch to join him in his office. Nothing was said as they walked to his office, and when the door closed the mayor indicated that he wished for them to sit. Before Butch could explain their presence there, the mayor began to speak.

"I received a personal call from General Tecumseh Brown this morning, so I know why you are back in town, and why you are in civilian attire. I am in agreement with the general that you should finish the mission that you began a short time ago. He has agreed to keep his security people in place until the mission is completed successfully."

"How are they working out, Mayor?" Claire asked. "Are they competent and fitting into the lifestyle of the City of Ashburn?"

"As far as competence, they are excellent. They are a bit intimidating to the general population, but I'm not so sure that that is not a good thing, at least temporarily. Our B&E incidents are non-existent since they came to town. No bar fights, no petty thefts at the local stores, and overall crime is down to almost zero. So, having them here is sufficient until you two complete your mission, whatever it may be, and return to us."

"Did the general tell you anything about our investigation and why we are still needed in the task of bringing the perp or perps to justice?"

"No, he simply said it was a matter of National Security, and that he could not elaborate on the details. I'm assuming you are under the same pledge to hold your investigation facts as top-secret data, and not allowed to share that with anyone outside the U.S.A.F. investigation."

"That is a good assumption on your part, Mayor. However, I will tell you that we spoke to POTUS briefly about the importance of this investigation, so as you can understand, this goes to the very top of the U.S. Government administration."

"You spoke to POTUS in person?"

"More or less. We were ushered into a special room in the Pentagon, and we spoke to the President indirectly through a video conference call. He is aware of our investigation, and he is concerned that our National Security may be at risk if we cannot determine exactly what happened to Flight C5-SGM12, the giant U.S.A.F. aircraft that crashed near the Joint Base Charleston. That's why we feel compelled to continue in our mission, now as civilian detectives, until we determine if the breach of security was due to foreign influence or national interference. At this point, we just don't have enough evidence to point either way."

"Mayor, Butch and I really love our jobs here, and we would like to think that this interruption will not reflect negatively upon our future career opportunities with the Ashburn Police Department."

"Claire, I'm a patriot. I served in the U.S. Army in the first Iraq War, and anything we can do as a community to support our military and the integrity of the U.S.A., we will gladly perform. You and Butch will be missed, but you must do your duty to this country and the mission you have accepted. I know it's top-secret in nature, but if you need any support from my office or the Ashburn Police Department, just let us know and we will be right by your side." The mayor rose from behind his desk, offered his hand to Butch and Claire, and indicated that the session was over. As they walked back to their apartment Butch looked respectfully at his partner.

"That was very impressive, Claire. Finding out exactly where the mayor and the city council stands gives us new viability in our quest for the truth. Well done!" Claire only smiled at Butch, and they continued their walk toward their apartment.

PART II: CORALING THE SLIPPERY ENEMY

Chapter 10

A New Approach

While Butch and Claire appreciated the authority granted them in their investigation on the Joint Base Charleston facility, real detective work was not usually something that took place in front of witnesses and out in the open. Butch and Claire had operated in the past much more successfully using subtlety, disguise, and misdirection to determine guilty parties and the crimes they were being charge with. Once Butch and Claire could determine, within a reasonable doubt, who the criminal mastermind was behind the downing of Flight C5-SGM12, they would use stealth to undercut any alibi or subterfuge that their opponent might be using to evade the truth.

"Do you play chess, Claire?"

"I have at times, but I must admit that I'm not very good at it. Why?"

"I want you to think of what we are doing in our private investigation of the crash as a type of 'Chess Trap.' '*Chess traps are moves which may tempt a chess opponent to play a losing move. Traps are common in all phases of the game.'*

That's pretty much the definition of a Chess Trap in Webster's Dictionary—entrapment that is performed so precisely that even if the opposing player knows what the chess master is doing, he or she cannot avoid falling into the trap."

"And what makes you so sure that our unnamed suspect will not recognize the chess trap and avoid making the fatal mistake of falling into the trap unaware of the danger?"

"The gambit is that the suspect *will* recognize that we are closing in on him or her, and he will flaunt his superior knowledge and intelligence and show us how he can play us without getting nabbed for the crime. It's the motivation behind the chess trap—the player being teased or tempted knows what's going on, but he believes he can outmaneuver or outsmart his opponent. Given the probability of success in the historical chess moves, the tempted player is like a fly who flaunts his ability to fly close to the spider's web, knowing that he can evade the spider by simply flying away when danger approaches. What he doesn't calculate is that there is little space for error—one false move and he's dinner for the spider. Genetic instinct probably alerts the fly to the danger, but confidence in past experiences overrides that caution and costs the fly his life. That's the gambit that I'm counting on."

Butch and Claire had arrived at home, they both kicked off their shoes, got a cold beverage from the refrigerator, and walked outside to the porched where they sat under a ceiling fan. They had to rethink everything now. They no longer had any unusual authority, like they did when Butch was an active colonel in the U.S.A.F. and Claire was a Special Agent for the U.S. Government. Now, they were simply two detectives with good experience at bringing perps to justice. They just hoped it would be enough to help them solve the mystery of the crash of Flight C5-SGM12, and what the reason was behind it. Butch took a long pull at his iced-cold beer, sat the bottle down on a small table, and appeared to look into the eternal blue sky that was favoring Ashburn today.

"Where do we begin?" Claire asked as she sipped on a wine cooler. "I'm not sure where we start our investigation."

"If the crime is not one of passion or revenge, one always should follow the money," Butch said.

"How do we know that this is not a crime of revenge or passion?"

"Good question. Claire. However, there are some basics that we should keep in mind. First, if a crime is committed by someone to gain satisfaction from a wrongdoing, there are usually indicators that the crime was motivated by those things—burning down a house of a successful businessman who treated his employees poorly; murdering a spouse after years of accepting abuse at their hands and doing nothing about it; or, taking valuables from a house when breaking in with the intent to steal from someone wealthier than most of his neighbors—these are crimes motivated by personal vendettas, in most cases. If someone was angry with the U.S.A.F. or the U.S. Government, why choose a particular flight and cause the crash, killing eight innocent airmen? This appears to me to be much more than a personal vendetta against a pilot or anyone else on Flight C5-SGM12. This crime has National Security implications written all over it."

"Assuming you're correct, how do we go about getting to the real reason someone wanted to bring down that jet? Obviously, poisoning the pilots would indicate that there's more to the crash than personal hatred of one particular individual, but where do we go from there?"

"We first need to determine if Captain Marshall Allgood was really part of the U.S.A.F., and if he was, did he survive getting off the airplane, and furthermore, who helped him accomplish that feat? That really is our only firm lead at this time."

"I think we may need for you to call Colonel Summers and get him to authorized us to have access to whatever records we deem necessary to continue our investigation. We may no longer be directly linked to the U.S.A.F. or the Pentagon, but we appear to still be working for General Brown and POTUS."

"Good point. I'll call him." Butch picked up his cell phone, dialed the phone number on the business card that the colonel had given him, and waited for his assistant to connect Butch with Colonel Summers.

"How may I help you, Butch?" the question came over his cell phone. It was obvious to Butch that the colonel appeared to be more congenial than when they had met him in General Brown's office. He had put his phone on speaker so Claire could hear the complete conversation.

"You probably know by now that General Brown has approved my final retirement from the U.S.A.F., but that my associate and I are still working on the case of the downing of Flight C5-SGM12."

"That's what I was told. He also told me that you and your associate gave credible evidence that the crash was not caused by suicide, as earlier diagnosed by the OAFME. Of course, any specifics of your investigation is on a 'Need to Know' basis, and I obviously don't need to know."

"Suffice it to say, Colonel, that our investigation generated more questions than answers, other than the fact that Lt. Colonel Ralph McGee, nor his co-pilot Major Buddy Hawkins, had anything to do with the downing of Flight C5-SGM12. They were victims as much as the remaining crew members and the giant aircraft. What we do need immediately is all the information that you can glean on a Captain Marshall Allgood, reportedly acting as the flight engineer on Flight C5-SGM12. We would like his personnel records searched, enlistment background check, and any suspicious activity the captain may have demonstrated while on duty in his entire military career. Do you think you can get that information for us pretty quickly?"

"I'll see what I can do. Having General Brown behind our requests should ease them through the red tape process better than if we were just making the requests ourselves. I have yours and your associate's business cards on my desk. Are the cell numbers still good for communications?"

"Yes, Sir. Just call or text me and I'll find a secure line and call you back. I don't trust that a cell phone communication can be totally secure with all the electronic surveillance possible these days."

"Right you are, Butch. Give me the remaining part of today, and I should have some type of answer for you by 0900 hours tomorrow morning."

"Thank you, Colonel. We appreciate your support." The colonel hung up without further comment, and Butch took the phone off speaker and consulted with Claire.

"And so, it begins," she said with a smile.

"And so, it begins," he agreed, took another long pull of his cold beer, and looked off into the deep, blue sky.

* * *

Butch and Claire sat on the porch for about an hour, letting everything that had transpired the past week filter through their new knowledge of being private investigators once more. There was less authority, but they could do things undercover that would have been impossible for Butch to have done in full, dress military uniform. The morning had lapsed into early afternoon, and Butch suggested that they celebrate their civilian status once more but having dinner at The Club in Homewood.

"That sounds nice, Butch. Can you get us in on this late a notice?"

"If Harold Simpson desires to fly second-seat at Mach 2.0 ever again!" Harold Simpson was The Club manager, and Butch had agreed to take him up in an F-16B fighter jet on a monthly basis in lieu of unlimited privileges at The Club. Butch had been faithful in his promise to Simpson, and The Club manager had done the same for Butch. Butch once claimed that he could get into The Club without a reservation on Christmas Eve and New Year's if he so chose to do so. It was good to have inside privileges in such a beautiful restaurant.

"How soon will you know if we can go? I'll need to get ready."

"Let me call him now," Butch said and dialed his friend. He gave Claire the 'thumbs up' signal, and she bounded into the bathroom to get prepared for a special night out on the town.

Butch and Claire had had some romantic encounters, but it wasn't an automatic or every night thing. They enjoyed each other's company just about as well as going to bed together. However, on special occasions, they woke up together in the same bed wrapped in each other's embrace. They were both young, unencumbered, and committed to living single as long as they desired, feeling no pressure from their peers or friends to either tie the knot or move away from each other. It was a good arrangement for both of them. They also rarely had time outside of their personal professional lives to date or meet socially with members of the opposite sex. There were no permanent ties, and they had agreed that dating someone else was acceptable in their relationship. The simple fact was that those occasions rarely happened. However, they enjoyed going out together and as long as that was the case, there really was no need for other people to date.

Butch was ready to go around 5:00 PM, but he had to wait for Claire to put the finishing touches on her makeup and hair. She came out of the bedroom sporting a little black dress, black pumps, and a simple strand of pearls. Her hair had been put up into a sophisticated bun, and she looked as pretty as Butch had ever remembered seeing her. He was dressed in a navy-blue sports coat, gray slacks, and a light blue silk tie.

"Are you ready for the big city?" Butch asked Claire.

"As ready as I will ever be," she said. They got into Butch's pickup, got on I-65 South, and headed for Homewood. They made small talk about the upcoming investigation and how they might approach things a little differently from the way they had while in the employment of the U.S.A.F. As Butch drove up Red Mountain on Richard Arrington Jr. Boulevard, he could see the imposing figure of Vulcan, the Roman god of fire and forge, holding his right arm high with a green light beacon, with his backside uncovered and mooning the small City of Homewood to the south. The Club was located down the ridge from Vulcan, just beyond the local NBC News outlet Channel 5, and overlooking the Southside of the City of Birmingham to the north and west.

"Butch, why didn't they put pants on that huge iron man's butt when they erected it?" Claire asked innocently.

"Claire, the City of Birmingham didn't forge Vulcan. The statue was created by the Italian artist, Giuseppe Moretti, and was created for the 1904 World's Fair in St. Louis, Missouri. It was then disassembled, moved to the City of Birmingham, Alabama, reconstructed, and placed atop Red Mountain, one of the mountains that ring the Southern slopes of the Appalachian Mountain chain. The City of Birmingham lies in the valley of that mountain chain, and the Vulcan statue stood atop the mountain for many years until the foundation below the massive structure began to give way and crumble into the foothills below. The pedestal was built to hold the 56-foot tall, 50-ton statue, and it stands 124 feet above the ground before the statue was added to the top, making the statue and tower a whopping 180 feet tall! So, the pants were a second thought, principally organized by several ladies' groups in the City of Homewood."

"You're joking, right? They were going to make Vulcan pants of some kind?" Claire began to laugh.

"Deadly serious, Claire. The project fell through when the feat became unachievable, but they *really* wanted to cover Vulcan's buttocks, for the children's sake." Claire began to laugh uncontrollably, and Butch joined her.

"I'm glad there are more important things to consider these days, like the tyrant in North Korea, the Chinese military growth, Russian involvement in everything to do with our country, and saving the whales."

"Saving the whales?" he mocked.

"Just thought I'd throw that in to see if you were listening. Anyway, it appears we have arrived at our destination!" Claire remarked as they pulled into the parking lot of The Club.

While Butch's pickup truck was clean and shiny, it still looked out of place among the Mercedes, Volvos, BMWs, and an occasional Rolls Royce Silver Ghost, that were visible in The Club's parking lot. Butch paid no mind, handed the keys to his beloved pickup truck to the parking attendant, and they moved inside the restaurant.

"Mr. Todd," the maître d said to Butch. We have reserved a nice table overlooking the Southside of Birmingham for you and your guest. I'll seat you now if you're ready." Mike indicated that they were indeed ready, and they were shown to one of the best tables in The Club.

"It must be nice having friends in high places," Claire said. "I guess this is one of the perks of having arrived in one's profession."

"Don't kid yourself, Claire. The only reason I can even get into this joint is due to my ability to take the general manager up in a supersonic airplane and scare the hell out of him once a month." Claire laughed at Butch's concise answer to her question.

"Well, there is that!" she agreed. "When are you going to take me up into the wild blue yonder, Butch? You haven't offered a ride and we definitely are closer than you and Harold Simpson!"

"I'll take you anytime you wish to go. In fact, I have a slot reserved for this weekend. Want to go?" Faced with the reality of flying in a two-seater jet at speeds exceeding the sound barrier, Claire was hesitant to answer. "If you don't want to go, I'm sure Harold would love to fly second-seat."

"I'll go. But you have to promise me that you will not kill us."

"No promises, but I will do my best to preserve both of our lives. We have a big case to solve and no one else to help us." Butch chuckled at being cavalier when it came to life-and-death decisions.

"How did you do that for nine years?"

"What?"

"Fly a machine that could very well end your life in a matter of seconds if something went wrong."

"Well, to be perfectly honest, there are very few times when the aircraft fails to perform as designed. It is usually pilot error that causes most crashes."

"Like in the crash of Flight C5-SGM12?"

"Even more so. The training jets that I fly are checked regularly by qualified mechanics, inspected before and after a flight, and go through a rigorous process of metal stress testing, engine performance, and things like that. You can imagine the complicated support that a C5 bird would attract. As I said in the beginning, very few military aircrafts crash because of malfunctioning parts or lack of maintenance on the aircraft. Almost all military aircraft crashes in peacetime are due to pilot error, or possibly something more sinister."

"Which brings us back to sabotage and/or treason on the part of someone on that aircraft who left during the flight."

"I would agree that it appears so, but we need to determine exactly who Captain Marshall Allgood is and where he fits into the puzzle we are trying to solve."

The waiter came, brought a bottle of white wine, took their order, and left them to stare out at the setting sun over the Southside of Birmingham.

"Now, that's a lovely sight. Unfortunately, once one gets down and dirty in the neighborhoods of Southside does one really appreciate the beauty of seeing such a scene from afar," Butch said.

"Gee, Butch. You could be a poet in another life!" They clinked their wine glasses and had a good laugh. "They could call you the 'Flying Poet,' or something to that effect.

"I think not," he said. "I let those who have talent to write prose and poetry handle that part of society—I have crimes to solve!"

Their dinner came and it was lovely, as always. Rack of lamb, baby field peas, a medley of stir-fried vegetables, and a small Caesar salad with capers. The wine was perfect for pork, so Butch ordered a second bottle and they feasted as if they were members in good standing. As they were finishing dinner, Butch got quiet. It was obvious enough that Claire asked him if something were bothering him.

"What we are about to launch into could get pretty rough. These people play for keeps. They would no more be concerned about killing us than swatting at a mosquito. They are professional killers and traitors. Their loyalties are to money and the influence it can buy."

"And you are telling me this for what reason?"

"To remind you of how dangerous our mission is, and to give you an opportunity to get out while you can. I can do this alone."

"You cannot do it alone as well as you could with someone watching your back. Deny that's the truth."

"You have a good point, but it doesn't have to be you. I can get the general to lend me someone to assist me."

"Are you doubting my ability to back you up? Are you trying to get rid of me?" Butch reached across the table and took Claire's delicate hand in his. His hand was almost twice the size of hers, and he squeezed her hand gently.

"No. I just don't want you to get hurt or worse."

"That makes two of us. Now, get to the plan. I'm not going anywhere."

They sat in the dining room that had possibly the best view of Birmingham over any other restaurant in the city. Butch had thought out many of the details of moving forward, with and without the U.S.A.F.'s assistance. Claire made suggestions when she thought it was appropriate, and by the time they had enjoyed dessert and were heading back to Ashburn, they felt pretty good about their approach to solving the reasons behind the crash of Flight C5-SGM12. They got home late, dressed for bed, and slept the sleep of the dead until the alarm clock woke them at 7:00 AM the next morning.

Chapter 11

Secret Files

"Where would one begin to look for 'missing files' that were created from an ongoing investigation of a military nature?" Claire asked.

"A super-secret server? You seem to be suggesting that there may be an undercover, secret investigation going on and we are not privy to the results. What makes you think such a thing is happening?""

"Besides being naturally suspecting of any U.S. Government investigation and its objectivity?"

"I see your point. However, right now we only have our suspicions and no hard facts to back up any potential conspiracy theories. What we need to determine is whether isolating the flight deck and the black boxes is standard procedure, or if a special effort was made to keep unauthorized eyes from looking at all the facts of the crash. One thing we need to keep in mind is that this was a classified, military exercise, and all the data and information surrounding such a crash would be handled differently than a civilian crash under similar conditions."

"That's also true, but if the Chief of Staff for the U.S.A.F. and POTUS authorized our investigation, isn't that the top of the military food chain? Where would one go to get a higher authority than they?"

"Have you ever heard of 'the Swamp' in Washington?"

"Foggy Bottom?"

"That term is probably appropriate when investigating something like this crash. There has always been the supposition that there is a shadow government infrastructure that every President and other high-ranking government official has to eventually answer to. Supposition has it that the shadow government was created to prevent a collapse of the public institutions, Congress, and any crisis that might cause the ultimate collapse of the free enterprise system of the United States."

"Which political party controls the establishment in Washington? Does it change as different administrations are ushered in, or is it independent of such influences?"

"Well, the fact that it is a 'shadow government' operation, little is known about how it operates, other than the commitment to the continuation of the freedoms we expect from any administration as they come and go over time."

"Is that realistic? Who doesn't have an opinion of whether we should do something, conservatively or liberally, speaking? It's my understanding that the shadow government was established by none other than George Washington in his first term as the President of the United States."

"Really? Do you believe such nonsense?"

"To be honest with you, Claire, I don't know what I believe. The grassy knoll in Dallas, men landing on the moon, the Bay of Pigs in Cuba—all these things have a mysteriousness about them that can't be easily answered. Did MLK, Robert Kennedy, George Wallace, President Kennedy, or even Abraham Lincoln meet their ends the way we were told? Who knows for sure? Things of this magnitude could have been effected by a secret society operating at the behest of the U.S. Government, couldn't they?"

"I guess that's possible, but doesn't that make you a conspiracy theorist?"

"I've been suspected of being worse than that, and definitely called worst!"

"Do we presume that there is a secret organization that goes all the way to the top as we endeavor to solve the cause of the crash of Flight C5-SGM12, or do we ignore such a possibility?"

"Let's just say that we need to remain openminded."

"In other words, trust no one!"

"Exactly!"

* * *

Butch and Claire had showered, dressed, and had consumed a simple breakfast with black coffee to give them some sustenance to help them maintain their energy for the day's work ahead. Claire was still unsure about how to begin their new search for the truth of the crash of Flight C5-SGM12.

"Since we didn't accomplish much at the Joint Base Charleston, where do we go from here?" Claire asked.

"What makes you believe we didn't accomplish much in Charleston?" Claire looked at Butch as if he had two heads.

"Well, correct me if I'm wrong, but the black boxes give us the only clues we have to follow about something amiss with the pilots' health and the possible missing flight engineer."

"You are correct about those two factors, but this is where detectives make their careers and livelihood. We actually have three leads—the poisoning of the pilots, the disappearance of the flight engineer, and the apparent attempted coverup of the event by the U.S.A.F."

"Those are challenging leads, Butch. Do you think we have enough leverage to get the appropriate doors open to us where we may sift through files and crash material enough to find the answers?"

"Now you may be seeing why General Brown chose us to investigate. He knows that the military investigative office will obey the rules of the game if the upper command tells them to button up the investigation and find a certain cause of the crash and death of the crew. The general probably read my personnel file and decided that besides my jet aircraft experience, and our private investigative skills, that I have been insubordinate more times than can be counted on both hands, using all the fingers and thumbs!"

"Meaning that you will not be scared away by some imposing authority, but rather will push the investigation as far as it will go under less-than-ideal circumstances?"

"Yep. I think the general has done a little research on Butch Todd, and in a pinch will come to our rescue if we get in over our heads with the U.S. authorities. He can't state that or put it in writing, but I'm counting on him if we really need him to bail us out."

"The alternative if he doesn't?"

"Leavenworth prison?"

"Swell."

"What we need to do next is generate enough interest in our investigation so someone makes a discernable mistake which we can act upon."

"What did you have in mind?"

"I'm putting a call in to Colonel Summers and asking him to get us everything in the government files on Captain Marshall Allgood—where he was born, his educational background, the security clearance files, and his prior duty stations."

"What if Captain Marshall Allgood was a fictitious character, and the possibility that he really doesn't exist?"

"Someone who was in the cockpit was identifying himself as Captain Allgood. It's possible that Allgood was not really 'Allgood,' but an impostor of some sort. Either way, there will be ways to document who was actually in the flight engineer's seat when Flight C5-SGN12 left the tarmac at Joint Base Charleston. It would be nice to have fingerprints of the perpetrator, but those are probably lost forever in the debris of the crash. However, the security of the U.S.A.F. for top secret missions, like the one Flight C5-SGM12 was performing, is very tight. Retina scans, fingerprints, and full-body scans are not unusual for the flight crew and the maintenance crew preparing such a flight. Colonel Summers can help us tremendously in that area, and we will get to work on background investigations into the captain and co-pilot of Flight C5-SGM12. We need to discover whether or not they were susceptible for possible blackmail or other pressures from outside sources. What really bothers me is that we have no idea what the mission of Flight C5-SGM12 was that day."

"I thought it was a simple training mission—touch-and-goes and routine flying exercises."

"Maybe yes, but maybe no. Ask yourself this question. 'Why would someone want to crash a multi-million-dollar aircraft and take eight crewmen down with it unless the mission was very important or damaging to someone else?'"

"What you're suggesting makes a lot of sense. What's our next logical step in the investigation?"

"After I place a call to Colonel Summers, we need to pack for a return trip to Charleston. This time I imagine we will be there for more than one or two days."

"Great! I love the historic nature of the city and its fine restaurants. Maybe we can eat at least one time at all of them before we leave."

"Hardly," Butch laughed. "There are hundreds of fine restaurants in Charleston, but we will do our best to visit as many as possible while we are there."

"Can we get the U.S.A.F. to pay for some of our expenses?"

"That's something I will cover with the colonel when I speak to him shortly. If what I think is going on is really happening, the general will authorize as much expense as is necessary to get to the bottom of this strange crash."

"Let's hope so."

Butch made the call to Colonel Summers, haggled about expenses, more authorization into restrictive files, and other specifics that Butch and Claire needed answered before they could move forward with the investigation. Once finished with the call, Butch told Claire that they were good to go and that most doors would be open to them when they needed the assistance."

"Most? Are there some we may need to address otherwise?"

"Let's cross that bridge when we get to it. Right now, we can log into the supercomputer at the Pentagon that holds all the records for enlisted and commissioned military personnel on active duty, and any other service personnel who have been on active duty in the past fifty years."

"Are we going as 'military conscripts,' or are we going back to Charleston as civilians?"

"Both," was his only answer. Claire hated it when Butch was so clipped in his responses because she could not tell read his moods when he communicated in such short answers.

"Would you kindly elaborate?"

"The general is sending us some civilian credentials which should open just about any door we need help with. The way the colonel described it was that the credentials carried the weight of his office, without the baggage of a chain-of-command."

"I hope you understand what that means, because I am lost in military language, especially vaguely intended innuendos."

"Trust me, they will help."

"The last time a man told me to trust him, I had to pull my chrome revolver and remind him that consent is given, not taken."

"Yikes! I'll try to remember that!" They both smiled at each other which tended to lighten the mood a bit. "The general said we could pick up the new credentials at the Joint Base Charleston. He is suggesting that we get Major Bennington to fly us directly to the base, without making a stop at Charleston International Airport. He will use his influence to get that flight scheduled so all we have to do is go to the 117th Wing Command at the Birmingham Airport and get on a jet."

"Will be it as comfortable as the last flight?"

"To be honest with you, Claire, I have no idea. It could be a G-7 or a Huey helicopter."

"Huey helicopter? I'm not familiar with that terminology. Is that military lingo?"

"Very much, indeed! That's just about the only efficient transportation that was available in Vietnam back in the mid-1960s and early 1970s. Not fancy, but real dependable. Most of them flew about 2000 feet off the ground at an airspeed of 140 knots. Oh, and they had no doors or seats."

"What? You don't think they would put us on something like that to fly us to an important mission, do you?"

"You never know about the government," was his only reply.

"Get me a seat inside a pressurized cabin or I'll skip the trip!" He just smiled and began packing his duffle bag.

* * *

They flew on a G-7 to the military airfield, were whisked away by an undercover secret service person once they had landed and were delivered promptly to The Gaslight Inn's front door. The concierge put their bags on a cart and rolled it into the lobby while they checked into the historic hotel.

"Ah, you're back," Allen said as he searched his computer for their reservation. "I see that Uncle Sam made your reservations and is picking up the tab this time. Nice." It was nice, because just the cost of the room and amenities The Gaslight Inn offered was more than their per-diem expense account allowed.

"Got to love Uncle Sam," Butch said and winked at Allen. "May we get the same two rooms—105 and 106?" Allen looked at the register and confirmed that they were becoming available after 2:00 PM. "If you want to walk to a restaurant and get a bite of lunch, we can have your things in your room by 3:00 PM. Will that work for you?"

"Sure. Do you have any recommendations for lunch? We ate at 82 Queen last time and it was its usual, wonderful self. I told Claire we would try something different this trip."

"You might try Blossoms on Church Street. They serve a fine seafood platter, along with other delights for lunch."

"Claire has informed me that she wants to eat at all the good restaurants in Charleston before we return home."

"Then I'd suggest you buy a home instead of staying in a hotel," Allen laughed. "Claire, there are at least 300 well-established, fine restaurants in the Battery area of Charleston alone. That doesn't include the ones on James Island, Johns Island, in Summerville, or the beaches. By my calculations, if you eat at a different restaurant three times a day until you have mastered the restaurant scene, you will have been in Charleston about four months. It would be fun trying something like that, assuming you are independently wealthy."

"I think we will just take it one restaurant at a time," she said. "I don't want to be thought of as 'Miss Piggy.'"

"That's a good plan, Claire," Butch said, taking her by the arm and leading her out the door to the side garden of the hotel. Do we need reservations for Blossom's for lunch?"

"I will call ahead for you, but usually there is little or no wait for lunch for most of the restaurants in Charleston. Dinner is another thing altogether. Do you need a reservation for dinner?"

"Yes. We will try Henry's, assuming you can get us in on such short notice. See if we can get a 7:00 PM seating."

"I will. I'll leave a message on your phone if I'm out when you return. Enjoy your lunch." Butch and Claire crossed over Meeting Street and began walking down Market Street. He reminded her where Anson's was located, and he then pointed out that Henry's was just across the square on the north side of the small road that separated the general market area from the restaurant. They walked briskly down Market and took a right on Church Street. Blossom's was just two blocks south on Church street, and there were no patrons waiting in line for lunch. The breezes were blowing across the peninsula, so Butch suggested that they eat outside in the small garden area attached to Blossom's. They were seated immediately, and Butch ordered them glasses of white wine from the waiter who sat them.

The waiter came back by the table shortly and Butch asked Claire if she would like for him to order for her. She said she would like some shellfish or something else light for lunch, and that she intended to feast at Henry's for dinner. Butch ordered She-crab soup for two, a shrimp salad, and hot, homemade bread with butter. Claire smiled and apparently agreed with his food choices since she didn't suggest anything different. They were sipping their wine when Butch began to lay out their upcoming plan of investigation.

"How are we going to play it differently this time to make sure we get farther along in our investigation. The last time we got shut down quickly," Claire asked.

"The last time we had to play by the rules because we were representing the U.S. Air Force. This time we are going to freelance a bit more."

"Forgiveness is easier to get than permission?"

"Something like that. Look, the government has not been honest with us in many things. We will simply play their game, and we'll take our chances."

"And if we get caught? Who is going to bail us out of the pokey?"

"Let us hope we don't get caught, and if we do, I will make a call to our favorite general. After all, he hired us back on a private investigatory basis—nothing official. And you heard me tell him that we would be calling him if we needed his help."

"I say we go for it. I've never spent the night in jail!" Claire smiled at him and Butch was reassured that this woman he had teamed up with was his equal when it came to rolling the dice. He was not sure that was a good thing, but it was the reality of the situation.

"You asked about the plan—here is stage one. We go to Base Charleston and use our detective credentials and the written order the general gave us to get onto the base and into the secure compound. Once inside, we play it by ear."

"That's your plan? Really?"

"You have a better idea?"

"Not really, but 'bobbing and weaving' is not what I call a great plan."

"Agreed. Let us finish lunch and we can go back to the hotel and prepare for tomorrow." Claire agreed. Their lunch came and Claire said that the she-crab soup was the best she had ever had. Butch had a dozen oysters, seafood gumbo, and more wine.

"Do you think you're going to get lucky tonight?"

"Lucky?"

"The oysters?" She smiled her best devious smile that she could muster.

"You never know—luck is my middle name!"

"And all this time I thought it was Butch!"

After lunch, Butch insisted that they walk down Church Street to Broad Street, south on Broad to Meeting Street, and east on Meeting Street until they reached Battery Park. Claire was impressed that the cannon balls were still present from the time the Battle of Charleston had been fought between the North and South. Butch pointed out that the structure on the horizon that they could see off the coast was Ft. Sumpter, the location of the first official battle of the Civil War. He also indicated to Clair where the canon ball had struck the steeple of St. Philip's Church, tilting is a bit from being perfectly horizonal with the other buildings on the street.

"There is so much history in this city," Claire gushed. "I would like to have been around back then—wearing hooped skirts and being fanned on plantation front porches, while sipping on sassafras tea."

"Have you ever thought that you might be the one operating the fan?"

"Never crossed my mind," she quipped.

They walked back up Meeting Street, went north on Broad, and took a right on King Street. Butch was patient as Claire window-shopped all the way back to Market Street where they took a right to return to Meeting Street and the Gaslight Inn.

"I'm beat!" Claire declared as she plopped down on one of the queen-sized canopy beds. "I think I'll take a nap before dinner."

"I have a better idea."

"What?"

"Why don't we get into the Jacuzzi in the courtyard, enjoy the muscle-relaxing heat, take a shower, then take a nap before dinner?" He raised an eyebrow when he asked the question.

"It's the oysters, isn't it?" Butch blushed a little but said nothing. Claire began to put on her bathing suit, so Butch assumed that she was in agreement with his plan.

When they stepped out of the room, the Jacuzzi was just a few steps away. The water temperature was 106 degrees, and initially the shock of the temperature jolted Claire. She sat on the side and dangled her legs into the foaming water. She slipped off the side and slipped under the water up to her neck.

"This is nice!" she said to no one in particular.

"I thought you'd like it. Fifteen minutes is probably enough to get rid of our aches and pains, don't you agree?" Claire gave Butch one of her most devilish looks.

"What I have in mind may create more of those aches and pains we just removed." She led him into their room and closed the door.

Chapter 12

Sleight of Hand

Butch and Claire climbed into the canopy bed—not to sleep, but rather to play. The Jacuzzi had put them both in a playful mood, and they further exhausted themselves before nodding off in one of the most comfortable beds Claire had ever slept in. Butch had left a wakeup call at the desk for 5:00 PM to make sure they had enough time to prepare themselves for dinner at Henry's. The last visit to Charleston had included a wonderful diner at Anson's—the crispy founder was to die for! As they walked toward Henry's, Claire asked Butch what to expect.

"Is Henry's the same type of cuisine as Anson's, or do they have a different approach to preparing their dishes?"

"Actually, Henry's and Anton's are similar, but different."

"Well, that comment is as clear as mud!"

"Not really. Where Anson's chef's approach to seafood is a true Lowcountry preparation, Henry's is more traditional and continental cuisine. If you get she-crab soup at Anson's you can expect sherry to be served alongside as a requisite for the dish to maintain its Low Country signature. Henry's also serves she-crab soup, but it is a hardier dish without the sherry. That's what makes Charleston's restaurants so unique. No chef approaches shrimp, crab, oysters, or fresh seafood filets in the same way. Whether you get shrimp, cod, salmon, or flounder for an entrée, every chef puts his signature on the dish to distinguish it from some other restaurant in the Battery. Speaking of Henry's, I like the way they approach beef wellington and other red meat dishes. It's difficult to find a perfect beef steak in Charleston since everyone thinks of seafood when they come to this city for dinner." They had walked east on Market Street, through the open market area, and were approaching Anson Street which would take them to Henry's.

"Wow! It's literally across the street from Anson's. How do two exclusive and expensive restaurants exist so close together in harmony?

"Millions of people come to Charleston and the Battery every year. This town lives on its appeal to tourists from all over the United States and the world. None of the exclusive restaurants seat more than thirty to forty people per seating, and they only have two or three seatings a night. Without a reservation we would be pressing our faces against the windows to even be able to see into these fabulous places." As they approached the door to Henry's, Butch held the door for Claire, and she stepped inside.

Claire immediately noticed the difference in the décor of the two restaurants. Anson's had been set up as a fancy, almost stuffy, exclusive restaurant with individual booths for parties of four or more, as well as small tables for parties of two. Claire saw it more like a ladies lounge and restaurant than a manly choice for dinner. Henry's, on the other hand, was very masculine with dark wooden floors, a hardwood bar that stretched the length of the room, and more substantial light fixtures and tables. If she had been measuring testosterone levels and comparing the two restaurants, Henry's would have won outright! She liked both settings. The more she visited the fine eating establishments of Charleston the more she loved the city overall. The waiter approached their table for their order. Claire had agreed to let Butch order dinner for her before they had entered the restaurant, so he ordered for both of them with no hesitation.

"For starters, bring us each a Henry's House Salad with shrimp, hot bread and butter, and a nice bottle of red wine. For dinner we will both have a grilled 12-ounce Ribeye steak with fresh local stir-fried vegetables. Cook my steak medium well and the lady's medium rare. And when you bring dinner, bring an order of crab cakes to share. Can you think of anything else you'd like, Claire?" She shook her head no and the waiter left.

"Wow! That's a lot of food. Do you think we can eat it all?"

"Sure," he said confidently. "And if there is anything leftover, we will take it back to the room in a 'go-bag' for a midnight snack."

"By the way, you never told me our arrangement with the general as to expenses on this trip." Butch pulled out a black American Express credit card and waved it discreetly at Claire.

"That has been taken care of by our sponsor. We are working for the U.S. Government, but we are private citizens with lots and lots of leverage when it comes to getting doors opened for us and passes into otherwise secret areas on Joint Base Charleston. I also have a letter of introduction available, when needed, if we are questioned or if someone tries to impede our investigation." He patted his sportscoat inside pocket for effect.

"I like the sound of that!" she cooed. "Let's spare no expense to get this investigation under way."

"My idea as well!"

Their salads were brought to the table, along with a bottle red wine as requested, and they began to dig into the wonderful food. They had just finished their salads and the waiter had cleared their plates when the steaks arrived, steaming on wooden carving blocks. Their steamed and stir-fried vegetables were added to the table and they began again in earnest with their dinners. As predicted by Claire, they couldn't finish everything, so Butch had the waiter put the remaining steak and totally untouched crab cakes in a 'go-bag,' Butch signed the check, and they waddled back toward the Gaslight Inn.

"I'm stuffed!" Claire said. "I should never have tried to keep up with you. You must have a hollow leg. How can you eat so much and never gain weight or seem to be affected by it?"

"Good genes, I guess," he laughed and put his arm around her as they made their way back through the market, now closed and boarded up for the night. "Let's walk off our meal by strolling down Market Street to the Battery. It's still light out and the streetlights will see us back to the hotel when we're ready to return. We will make a big circle of the Battery, return to Market Street by way of Church Street, and stop at Kaminsky's for a piece of chocolate cake on our way back to the Gaslight Inn."

"I couldn't eat another bite of anything, Butch!"

"After a brisk walk for twenty or thirty minutes you will want a piece of chocolate cake—especially Kaminski's chocolate cake!"

"OK. You may have to carry me home if I pass out along the way." Butch just smiled at his pretty partner. He figured she could probably drink him under the table if she were a mind to try it, but he let her have her fantasy of being a potential damsel in distress. They walked about two miles and wound up at Kaminski's around 9:00 PM. The party was just beginning to get cranked up at Kaminski's, with a jazz band and soul singer as the entertainment. They split a piece of chocolate cake, had coffee to help them wake up after the heavy meal at Henry's, and then they began their trek back to the Gaslight Inn.

"Want to take another dip in the Jacuzzi?" Butch asked. Claire looked at him as if he had two heads.

"No, Butch. I want to get out of these clothes, get into bed, and go to sleep. Nothing more—nothing less."

"Come on, Claire. Don't be a spoil-sport."

"Goodnight, Butch," she said after stepping out of her clothes, climbing into the big canopy bed, and falling asleep immediately as her head hit the pillow. He looked at her and was glad they had hooked up as partners and sometime lovers. However, he was too geared up to go to bed at 9:30 PM. He put on his swim trunks and headed for the Jacuzzi.

* * *

The sun was shining through the wooden shutters that covered the windows in Room 106, and the bright light was enough to stir Butch out of his light slumber. He looked at the clock on the end table near the bed and saw that it read 6:15 AM. A quick glance at his partner revealed that she was still in deep sleep mode, and not bothered at all by the light of morning. He slid out of the bed, made his way quietly to the bathroom, and surveyed the damage that their night on the town had done to his appearance. His appearance needed some serious attention, but he figured that a shower, shave, and a few cups of hot coffee would return his appearance to normal. As he brushed his teeth, he started the shower in preparation for his transition back to normalcy. Within a few minutes he was clean and dry and ready to dress for their big day at Joint Base Charleston. He had chosen a lightweight gray suit, white shirt, an understated tie, and he shaved and dressed quickly once he was back in the room in front of the vanity mirror. He heard stirring in the bed, and when he looked he saw Claire lying with her eyes open but otherwise appearing still and quiet.

"Good morning, Sunshine!" Butch said as he continued to look at himself in the mirror. It's 6:40 AM and we need to leave here around 8:00 AM to get to the base and start our investigation."

"I can't believe I overate, walked miles after dinner, and drank entirely too much wine last night. The last thing I remembered was stepping out of my clothes and climbing into bed. What time was that?"

"Approximately 9:30 PM. I had suggested another dip in the Jacuzzi, but you would have no part of it. You simply got into bed, and you've been asleep for over nine hours. You should feel rested."

"I feel as though I was hit by a Mack truck! I'll have to be more cautious tonight if we are to accomplish our goals while we are in Charleston. As it is I will be dragging around like I have an additional weight attached to my ass."

"And a nice ass it is, if I don't mind saying."

"I'm afraid to look in the mirror this morning. It may take me hours to repair the damage of last evening's events."

"You have about forty-five minutes. Good luck."

Claire rolled off the four-poster bed, padded to the bathroom, and shut the door. She told Butch to go down to the lobby and get his breakfast while she tried to repair the damage she involuntarily inflicted upon herself the night before. He left quietly, and she opened the bathroom door, stared into the vanity mirror, and shuttered. This was going to be a major project to get her appearance where she wanted it, so she jumped into the shower, washed her hair, dried herself thoroughly, and began the art of painting her face. In something just short of forty-five minutes she appeared on the patio by the lobby looking pert and pretty.

"Wow! I would never had believed you could do such an amazing job of getting ready in such a short period of time. Congratulations!"

"Shut up, and please get me a cup of coffee and a glass of orange juice." Claire smiled when she spoke to Butch, but he had no doubt that this was not a morning to tease his fellow investigator. He was back at the table with the requested items in a flash. He sat down, opened the local *Post and Courier* to the society page. He seemed absorbed into his reading, but he was simply trying to avoid any extensive questioning about their previous night's activities. Butch flipped to the business section and emitted a whistle from his mouth.

"What?" Claire asked.

"Look at this!" Butch slid the newspaper over so Claire could read the headline at the top of the business section. It read: *"The crash of the jet at Joint Base Charleston has been ruled an accident, and no ill effects are expected for the future of the base's operations."*

"When did that happen? I thought there had been no designation of the cause of the accident. That changes everything, assuming it is the official position of the U.S.A.F. Is there any way to check with General Brown's office to validate such a claim?"

"Sure. Let me call his office." Butch dialed the personal cell phone number that the general had given him for contacting him in cases such as this. After only a couple of rings, the general's voice came on the line. He obviously had phone recognition software on his cell phone, and he knew the caller was Butch.

"I saw it, Butch. I did not authorize that statement. However, now that it is out there in the public, I think we might use the misleading statement to our benefit." That comment took Butch by surprise. He had been ready to ask that the U.S.A.F. demand that statement from the *Post and Courier* be retracted, so he was taken aback by General Brown's comments.

"I think you've lost me, General. You want a lie to stay out in the public domain about something as important as possible espionage?"

"You're not following me closely, Butch. I want to use whatever is at our disposal to find the truth. We know that there was a third person, the flight engineer, in the cockpit of the aircraft before it crashed. We know he disappeared somehow since his body was never found in the wreckage. We have the flight recorder information that clearly defines that the crash was not an accident. What we don't have yet, and I emphasize *yet*, is who was really behind the crash and why did it have to happen? If the public thinks that the crash has been deemed an accident, they will ease up on the investigation process that every crash undergoes with the NTSB in such cases. Since the U.S.A.F. is the ultimate authority in its dealings with the press and the public, I am hoping those responsible for the misinformation will feel safe and secure, thinking that they are now above suspicion. That should make your job a bit easier. Don't you agree?"

Butch had to quickly consider everything that the general had just said to him. As far as taking the heat off their investigation was concerned, the general was correct. No one would suspect that Butch and Claire would find anything alarming or disquieting once the U.S. Government officially stated the apparent cause of the crash of Flight C5-SGM12. Butch could even see a sleight of hand move that might help them get to the bottom of this case much quicker if everyone thought that the case was officially closed.

"I think I see where you're going with this, General. Do you think we should modify our approach to the investigation at Joint Base Charleston?"

"Absolutely. Are you at a location where I can fax you something?"

"Yes, Sir. We are staying at the Gaslight Inn in Historic Downtown Charleston. Do you know the place?"

"Sure. I stay there from time to time when I visit Charleston. Is the innkeeper still the same one whose been there forever?"

"Yes, Sir. Allen Johnson has been the innkeeper at the Gaslight Inn for as long as I can remember, and I've been staying here for at least twenty years."

"Give him my warmest regards. He's a great innkeeper. Unfortunately, most hotel and motel managers today have lost the personal touch with their clients. Not Allen. He's the best!"

"I agree. However, tell me how you think we should alter our approach to the investigation at Joint Base Charleston now that the official word is out as to the cause of the crash?"

"Can you read me the fax number of the Gaslight Inn?" Butch had a business card of Allen's in his suit pocket, so he looked at it and repeated the number to the general.

"Are you sending us more instructions, Sir?"

"No, but I'm altering your mission statement. Just read the fax and tell me if you have questions. Otherwise, good luck!" The general hung up, and Butch realized that there had been a dynamic move in how the general perceived their investigation should proceed. He excused himself from the table, went into the inn's office, and asked Allen if he had received a fax addressed to Butch. Allen went back into the inner office and came out with a single sheet of paper showing a couple of printed badges and a short message. Butch thanked him, moved back to the patio where Claire was still recovering from last night's activities, and looked at the fax.

"We have new badges," he said quietly.

"New badges? Badges for what purpose?"

"They look like U.S.A.F. C.I.D. authorizations."

"Run that by me again. What do you mean C.I.D.? That's criminal investigation department, if I'm not incorrect."

"You are correct, but there is a twist. In the U.S.A.F. the C.I.D. Office carries a Special Investigation designation. We are officially privately commissioned Special Investigators for the U.S.A.F. According to the note attached to the badges, we are authorized to see all intelligence Information up to an including '*Eyes-Only*' material. That's the same level U.S. Senators, top Generals, and POTUS possess. With our current letter of authorization, along with these badges, we should be unstoppable when it comes to having our investigation requests granted by local authorities."

"Where do we go from here?"

"Let's go to a UPS or FED/EX store, get these badges laminated and more professionally created, and then we're off to Joint Base Charleston." Butch asked Allen where the closest UPS or FED/EX office was located that could create the kind of badges from the printout that the general had sent. Allen directed them to the FED/EX location at 73 St. Philips Street, just north of the College of Charleston campus. They went back to their room, got their briefcases, freshened up after their breakfast, and headed for their car which was parked a few blocks away in a designated parking lot that the Gaslight Inn used for its guests. When they arrived at the car they noticed that all four tires had been gashed with what appeared to have been a sharp instrument, like a knife. On the windshield there was a short statement written for their benefit. *"Go home. You are in over your heads, and the next warning may be terminal."*

When Claire saw the car she was stunned into silence. She had not expected personal attacks by the U.S. Government, or agents working for them, and it jolted her into the reality that they might actually be in over their heads.

"What do you think?" she asked as she turned to Butch who was standing observing the damaged vehicle.

"I think we're getting too close for comfort for some people. That's a good sign."

"A threat to our lives is a good sign?"

"From my experience as a detective, when people threaten to harm you they are simply trying to scare you off your mission. If they really intended bodily harm to us they would have shot first and asked questions later!"

"I'm guessing that means you don't intend to quit this investigation?" Butch looked at her incredulously. He wasn't sure if she were scared of continuing their search for the truth, or if she was just testing his determination to see this through to the bitter end.

"I know this could be dangerous, Claire. I can't guarantee that we will not be harmed in our continuation of this investigation, and for that reason I am willing to pursue this course of action on my own, if necessary. The only reason someone would try to scare us off our course of action is that they think we are getting too close to the truth. I've been cursed at, shot at, thrown into jail, beat up in public, and other things I won't describe to you for reasons of decorum. However, I have never, *never*, quit an investigation because of threats or potential danger to myself or others. That's why I am offering you an out. I will not hold it against you if you think you need to bow out of this investigation and return to Ashburn. We will resume our normal partnership when I return from this mission. Your choice."

"Mission, huh? That's what I thought. You see this as an extension of your military career as a fighter pilot—kill or be killed! All I want to know is if you think we have at least a 50% chance of success if we proceed, despite the possible dangers to our personal lives?"

"Claire, I can best describe my feelings by explaining the psychic mind of a fighter pilot. No fighter pilot, who is probably flying a multi-million-dollar aircraft, can think of possibly losing the fight. There is only one result acceptable, and that is winning! Every pilot is not successful, and some die or lose their aircraft, and have to eject to fight another day. If any pilot thinks he may lose a battle, he should not be flying the mission. The U.S. has the best aircraft technology in the sky, the best naval ships, the best radar, armament, supply lines—the works. However, what makes it all work is the superior mind of the U.S. aviator. So, to answer your question, my answer is that we have a 100% chance of success."

"I can tell you now that I am not going home without you. I'm not afraid of dying—dying is a part of life. All I wanted to hear is that you are convinced that if we do our jobs correctly we have a better than 50% chance of success. Is that what you're telling me?"

"More than that, Claire. We have to believe that we were put in this position by a force much larger than you or me, or even the general, to do what we can to preserve the integrity of the U.S. Government and its reputation. I see us as modern-day Nathan Hales. Whether or not Hales' often quoted line, "*I regret that I have only one live to lose for my country,*" is accurate or not, he was one of the first patriots of the newly constituted United States of America. He was an undercover spy at fourteen years of age, and he was hanged by the time he reached the age of twenty-one. But Hale, despite all the rumors, accolades, and criticism, was in it to win it. He was all in—not just a little—all in. I'm all in, Claire. And, if you're all in as well, I want you to stay. I'm a better detective with you as my partner, but you have to have the Nathan Hale attitude. We have to believe, like our forefather Patrick Henry, that liberty is worth the price of potential death by the enemy. Something very wrong is going on at very high levels of our government, and I intend to expose it. As I said before, the choice is yours. It might have a bad ending for you, me, or both of us. If that's the case, we will have gone into the battle with our eyes fully open."

"I'm fully in. By the way, has anyone ever suggested that you could be either a top recruiter for the military, or possibly the greatest salesman in history?" She gave him her warmest, convincing smile. He returned her smile with his own. They headed to the FED/EX office on St. Philip Street to create their official documents.

Chapter 13

Undercover Sleuths

Butch and Clair walked from the FED/EX office on St. Philip Street with confidence that their newly created badges gave them a credible identity as Special Investigation Agents of the U.S.A.F. Butch had gone online and discovered exactly how an agent's badge looked in real life, so he designed their badges as close to the original as possible. The signature on the badges was the authenticated version of General Tecumseh Brown, and no one was going to question at great length if it was real or not. Butch and Claire were carrying their firearms in a concealed manner, they both had concealed carry permits issued in the State of Alabama, and Butch doubted any military command officer or underling was going to demand that they surrender their firearms. Both Butch and Claire were excellent marksmen, with Claire actually outperforming Butch on most occasions at the firing range. He was happy to have such a qualified wing man, as he might describe Claire to anyone who asked about her qualifications. Now they needed transportation to the base that would present them in the best light. They needed a believable police-type vehicle, and Butch thought he knew where they might borrow one. He suggested that they walk down to the Four Corners of Law intersection. The City Hall was situated at Meeting Street and Broad Street, and Butch thought he might be able to convince an old friend to help him with his transportation needs. Butch had discovered a few years ago that one of his fellow U.S.A.F. flyers had taken a job with the mayor's office in Charleston as his Public Relations Director, and Butch had spoken to him a few times since he was hired. This was a great time to renew his acquaintance, because Butch remembered that his friend owed him a big favor.

"Let's walk down to City Hall. We need wheels, and not just any wheels, and I have a friend who may be able to help us get a vehicle that will make our trip to Joint Base Charleston more successful."

"Just who is this friend, and why would he feel obligated to help you?

"A few years ago, when I was flying missions in Afghanistan against the Taliban, I had a sergeant who worked on my jet when it was out of service and was being prepped for another mission. SGT Lawrence Ledbetter, a tech sergeant with a pay grade of E-6, had gone into town to party one night when we had a twenty-four-hour pass and off time to ourselves. He had gotten drunk, made a pass at a local waitress, and was going to be reported by the bar owner for sexual harassment and assault. I was in the bar that night and convinced the bar owner not to prosecute SGT Ledbetter for reasons that benefited the owners as well as the sergeant. If any U.S. Military person got into trouble in a local bar, that bar was off-limits for a minimum of thirty days after the incident. Obviously, that would have cost the owner lots of money. SGT Ledbetter agreed to apologize to the waitress, gave her 200 Afghani in currency, and promised to never enter that bar again. It probably saved SGT Ledbetter from getting sentence to a night in the brig and a ding in his personnel record, so he *owes* me." They began their walk from the FED/EX store toward city hall down on Meeting Street at the Four Corners of Law.

"How much is 200 Afghani?"

"Two-dollars and sixty cents!" Butch laughed as he remembered the story. He didn't bail out his friend for any reason other than Butch didn't want a stranger arming his jet fighter the next day. Now, it appears there was a silver lining in Butch's redemption of his tech sergeant.

"If you can parlay a $2.60 bribe into an official-looking ride for us while we are in Charleston, that will have to be the best illicit deal ever made!" They both chucked at her comments. They had walked past their hotel, the Historic Charleston City Market, Circular Congregational Church and its historic graveyard, The Mills House Hotel, and Washington Square before arriving at one of the most celebrated intersections in history—the Four Corners of Law. On these four corners county law, city law, federal law, and God's law all were represented by historic buildings which dated back hundreds of years. Butch and Claire climbed the long flight of concrete and marble stairs that led to the main entrance to Charleston City Hall. They entered the lobby and told the receptionist that they were there to see Mr. Larry Ledbetter. She looked down at the switchboard and called his office to see if he could see them. She indicated that Larry would come out to the lobby and get them, and she invited them to sit on a very uncomfortable looking bench while they waited.

"Larry?" Claire questioned Butch. "He goes by Larry and not Lawrence?"

"If you had a choice, which would you choose?"

"I see your point." A well-dressed man in his thirties came out of the back office and approached them with his big hand extended to Butch.

"How are you, Old Man?" Larry asked. "It's been quite a while since you've come to see me. And I see you brought a lovely young woman to make our visit together more pleasant." Larry introduced himself, kissed Claire's hand, and welcomed them both to Charleston.

"This young lady is Detective Claire Cavendish, my partner in our detective agency. We are here on official business, but I am glad to see you. I would have called ahead but our trip was not scheduled until yesterday. I hope we are not disturbing you too much."

"Oh, not at all," he gushed, looking at Claire and attempting to stare through her clothes all the way to her soul. Butch decided that SGT Lawrence Ledbetter had not changed much since their military days together in Afghanistan. "How can I be of assistance to you?" Larry actually seemed to mean his statement, and he expressed great interest in their visit with him. He invited them into his office, and they all took a seat—him behind a large desk, and they in front of the desk in straight back, wooden chairs with no cushions.

"I need a favor," Butch said. "I've never called in my chips for saving your butt in the bar in Afghanistan, but now I need something that only you can provide. Help me out and I'll consider our ledger even."

"That sounds rather ominous, Butch. What makes you think I have the authority to grant such a favor, and what is it exactly you need for me to do for you and the lovely Claire Cavendish?" He looked longingly at Claire again and her skin began to crawl with goosebumps. This guy was really a creep.

"I need a car for a few days, and I was hoping you could use your influence with the Mayor's Office to secure one for me."

"A car? Is that all? That's a pretty good swap to remove the debt you've been holding over my head for the past few years. What kind of car?"

"That's the tricky part. I don't need just any car, or I would rent one from Avis or Hertz. I need a Crown Vic that screams police cruiser as I drive down the street. Ideally, I want a big, black monster Crown Vic with black sidewall tires, a couple of antennae whipping around on the trunk, and a complete police cruiser package inside, replete with dashboard lights, a two-way radio, and a prisoner cage in the back seat. Oh, and a big, ugly crash bar mounted on the front bumper!"

Larry stared at Butch for a moment before answering. He started to speak, but instead picked up the desk phone and called someone. When the other party picked up, Butch could imagine the other end of the conversation as Larry made Butch's needs known. Larry hung up, stood up, and stuck out his hand.

"Done!" Larry wrote down an address on a notebook page, tore it out, and handed it to Butch. "This is the address of our automotive department, and you can get there by walking back up Meeting Street to Market Street, then turning right until you get to East Bay Street. Turn left on East Bay and about three blocks on the right you will find the Charleston Motor Pool. You will want to ask for Smitty—our chief mechanic. He will sign you out our best Crown Vic for a few days. Just remember if you wreck it you have to replace it!"

Butch took Larry's hand, shook it confidently, and began to leave the office. He was surprised that Larry had the gall to ask a favor in return.

"What kind of favor do you think I can grant you, Larry?"

"Oh, it's not you that I wish the favor from. I would like for Ms. Cavendish to have dinner with me tonight at Anton's. What do you say, Claire?" Larry smiled as he made his offer to her.

"Well, Larry, I guess the best thing for me to say to you is the truth. I don't wish to go to dinner with you. I don't know you, and I don't particularly like you. Also, I have a snub-nose, chrome-plated revolver in my purse that I am quite accurate with. If you made some move toward me that displeased me, I might blow your balls off in the restaurant, and I wouldn't want to have to do all the paperwork that such an evening might require. So, no, I will not have dinner with you. But thanks for asking." She turned on her heel and was out the door of his office and headed out of City Hall before Butch could catch up with her. Butch looked back at Larry as he left his office and tried to catch up to his partner. Larry was still standing behind his desk with a shocked look on his face. Butch caught Claire on the steps of the building as they descended to the main level of Broad Street.

"I guess that was unnecessary, but it felt good. I hope it doesn't spoil our opportunity to get the Crown Vic," Claire said as she continued to walk toward Meeting Street.

"No, I don't think that was a quid-pro-quo offer that had been made earlier by our host." Suddenly, Butch began to howl with laughter. "I believe Larry was convinced that you would do exactly what you said you would do if he tried to molest you in any way. The look on his face was priceless!" Claire looked back at Butch without any smile on her own face and made a simple statement that he believed to be true.

"That was not a bluff—I'd blow the bastard's balls off if he even suggested anything that I interpreted as sexual harassment. Believe it!" Butch nodded, and they continued to walk toward Market Street where they would turn right to get to East Bay Street and the Motor Pool. Without any outward sign to her, Butch admired Claire's fire and determination. She was definitely the right partner for something as dangerous as their current mission.

They arrived at the Charleston City Motor Pool after walking for approximately twenty minutes from City Hall. Since it was still morning, the day had not heated up to the point of suffocating humidity, and the winds blowing across the peninsula were still cool and light. Butch walked directly into the auto bays and looked for a grease-monkey with a uniform that had the name "Smitty" embroidered above the pocket of his shirt. He spotted him right away. Smitty was the typical head mechanic who had probably retired after serving twenty years in the Navy as a grease-monkey. He had huge arms and a broad back—he looked like a retired prize fighter without the flat, broken nose that accompanied most boxers when their time was up in the ring. Butch approached him and extended his hand in friendship.

"I'm Butch Todd, a friend of Larry Ledbetter down at City Hall. He said I should see you about borrowing a Crown Vic for a few days." Smitty held up his greasy hands in a show of consideration to not soil Butch or his clothes by shaking his hand. Smitty indicated for them to follow him into the office. Smitty washed his hands and then stuck his hand out to shake both Butch's and Claire's extended hands. "Did Larry call you about us?"

"Oh, yeah. The Crown Vic is not a problem," and Smitty pointed to a black sedan tricked out with every police option Butch could have wanted installed on it. "Just sign it out and try to bring it back in the same condition it is now."

"We will take great care not to damage it in any way. Did Larry say anything else about us?" Butch didn't know exactly why he wanted to ask Smitty that question, but he felt he needed to know the answer. Smitty looked down and looked a little embarrassed.

"Yeah. He said not to mess with the little lady, because she threatened to blow his balls off?" Smitty made the statement with a solemn look on his face, which prompted a look from both detectives. Claire spoke up and clarified her comments to Larry.

"Smitty, you seem to be a decent fellow. Larry kind of creeped me out while he and Butch were talking about their days in the Air Force, and when Larry made a less-than-gentlemanly gesture about taking me to dinner, I guess I just spoke my mind. Please don't hold it against us."

"Oh, you don't have to apologize to me. I know all about Larry Ledbetter. He thinks he's a ladies man, but most ladies don't want anything to do with him—like you. You both just be careful with this machine that I'm lending you. This is one of the last production Crown Vic's that came with the police interceptor package. It has a 215 HP, turbo-charged engine that will cruise at 135 MPH until it runs out of gas. It has oversized tires, a reinforced spring system and transmission, and it is almost indestructible. It weighs over two tons and is considered one of the toughest vehicles on the road in the police equipment category. The only vehicle I would prefer when chasing bad guys is an Abrams Tank!" Smitty laughed at his own joke, and Butch and Claire laughed with him.

"We will take good care of her, Smitty. We don't intend to get into any chases or other dynamic instances, but it's good to know this baby can handle what comes her way!"

"That's what they all say every day when my police units leave the motor pool—some come back undamaged, but some go straight to the salvage yard."

"I promise I'll make him drive carefully, Smitty," Claire said, winking at him as they drove away.

"You think you can influence how I drive a beauty like this?"

"Absolutely. In your case, the chrome-plated revolver is not the only threat I can use with you." Butch had to acknowledge that she had a good point, so he just shut up and headed the car up East Bay Street to the intersection where they could pick up I-26 North, which would take them to the Joint Base Charleston. The trip to the Charleston International Airport took twenty minutes, and they exited the freeway and drove around the fenced property of the airport to the entrance of the Joint Base Charleston. As they pulled up to the Marine standing guard at the gate, Claire saw the value of arriving in the Crown Vic.

"May I see your identification?" the gate guard asked Butch as they pulled alongside his station. Butch handed him both laminated passes which they had created with the fax they had received from General Brown. He stepped inside the little guardhouse, stepped back outside and returned their passes to them, and motioned them onto the base. For now it appeared the passes were working, and they both breathed a sigh of relief.

One thing that they had going for them was that they knew from their past visit to the base exactly where they needed to be to uncover any misinformation that had helped the U.S.A.F. to determine the crash of Flight C5-SGM12 was an accident. Butch pulled up to the second security gate that led to the highly protected secret hanger where they had first suspected a third person in the aircraft's cockpit on the day of its demise. Another Marine guard, this one with an Uzi machine gun, held his hand out for them to stop. He approached the car slowly, taking in the full effects of the black Crown Vic and its emphasis on being an official police vehicle, and asked for their credentials.

"We are on assignment from the Secretary of the U.S. Air Force, General Tecumseh Brown, and that's all you need to know, Sergeant," Butch answered the guard with authority. "We need access to that hangar," Butch pointed to the one from where they had been summarily dismissed just a week ago, “and we need access now!”

“Sir, do you have specific orders allowing you access to that hangar?” Butch pulled out the letter from General Brown, handed it to the Marine, and prayed that it would allow them access. The guard took the letter, read over it quickly, handed the letter back, saluted the automobile, and raised the gate to allow them full access to the site. As they pulled away from the guard shack Claire let out her breath slowly which she had been holding since the second guard had appeared.

“That was close,” she whispered, as if the guard might overhear her. “This is exciting!” Butch just looked at her and smiled. Claire Cavendish added lots of color to his normally boring investigations. “If I remember correctly, there are more guard ahead inside the hangar—right?”

“Yep, but that’s not going to be a problem this time. The letter that the general wrote indicated that we are not to be questioned on the substance of our visit. If anyone deems it necessary to stop and inquire about our authorization to be here they will have to deal with the general’s office personally. I can tell you from a military man’s perception in the past—that’s just not going to happen.”

They took their briefcases, put their sidearms in their holsters, and entered the hangar unobstructed. Butch recognized the area where they had been before and immediately moved toward the flight deck to see if anything had been changed from their last visit. Nothing seemed out of order, so he asked the guard where the data logs were being kept in reference to the recordings of the black boxes retrieved from the crash. Hesitating only briefly, the guard indicated to Butch that the keyboard on the desk next to the flight deck remains was where he would find the information he was searching for. Butch pulled up the file, made a copy of both black boxes recordings and placed it on a USB drive which he had put in his pocket before they left the hotel. Butch signed off the program on the computer, indicating to Claire that it was time for them to return to the Crown Vic. They walked out of the hangar, drove off the base, and headed back to the Gaslight Inn.

"Do you think we got what we needed with those recordings?"

"I think when we put these recordings up against the facts that someone was in the cockpit who wasn't accounted for after the crash, we will be well on our way to solving the mystery of why Flight C5-SGM12 had to be destroyed."

"Didn't you asked Colonel Summers to work up a complete background on Captain Marshall Allgood, the flight engineer who disappeared mysteriously before the crash occurred?"

"I did, and I think he's had enough time to come up with a comprehensive profile which could prove helpful to us. When we get back to the Gaslight Inn we will give him a call and get him to bring us up to date on his findings." Butch headed the Crown Vic back toward their hotel, doing his best to stay within the parameters of the speed limits on the freeways. It was difficult for him, because he really wanted to open the big roaring engine up to see what it could do on a straight away, but he didn't want to bring notoriety to themselves and their investigation if they were stopped for speeding in a City of Charleston vehicle. Butch pulled into the concierge parking spot in front of the Gaslight Inn, handed the keys to the parking attendant, and asked him to park the car close enough for them to retrieve it quickly, if necessarily.

"How was dinner last night?" Allen asked as they walked through the lobby toward the door that would take them to Room 106.

"Very nice," Claire said. "Unfortunately, I ate too much and fell asleep early. Henry's was a great choice for dinner!"

"Do you want a reservation for dinner tonight?" Allen asked.

"Yes, I think so. Why don't you surprise us!" Claire said. "Just leave a message on the room number and we'll pick it up later in the afternoon."

"Any particular cuisine you'd prefer this evening?"

"Low-Country seafood would be nice," Butch answered for Claire. She had already made the turn out the door of the lobby and was headed for their room.

"I have just the perfect restaurant in mind," Allen answered, picking up the telephone and dialing the restaurant for reservations. Slightly North of Broad, or SNOB, was considered another of the premier restaurants in the Battery area, and reservations were a little more difficult to get because the restaurant was a hometown favorite, as well as popular with out-of-town guests. Allen was successful in securing dinner reservations for 7:00 PM, and he called and left that message on the room telephone.

Claire had stopped at a table in the courtyard near the Jacuzzi to rest a moment and gather her thoughts. Butch brought a glass of white wine from the lobby bar for them to sip while they contemplated their next move.

"Why don't you call the colonel and put the telephone on speaker phone so I can hear both sides of the conversation?" Claire asked. "While the black box recordings may shed light that there were actually three people in the cockpit just before the crash, it will not tell us who that third person might be. I'm betting it is our mysterious flight engineer, Captain Marshall Allgood." Butch dialed the number for the general's office, asked for Colonel Summers, and waited patiently while he was being located, and the call transferred to his phone.

"Colonel Summers," was the response on the other end of the telephone connection.

"Colonel Summers, this is Butch Todd. Claire and I have made some inroads into the investigation that General Brown has assigned us to, but we need to get the background report on the flight engineer, Captain Allgood, that your people have worked up for us. Do you have that report handy?"

"Just a minute," he said, and the line went dead for a few minutes. Butch thought that their connection might have failed, and he was getting ready to redial the general's office when Colonel Summer's voice came back on the line. "Here it is," he said, as he thumbed through a stack of papers the Butch could hear him shuffling at his desk. "That's interesting. That's really interesting."

"What's interesting?" Butch asked expectantly. "Is it good news or bad news?"

"I'm not sure. I'll just fax this report to you and let you decide. The file is too long to discuss over the phone, so give me a fax number and I'll get this off to you immediately." Butch gave them the fax number for the Gaslight Inn and hung up the telephone. He walked back into the office and met Allen coming to deliver the fax he had just received.

"Thanks, Allen." Allen handed the fax to Butch and returned to the office. Butch took the document to the table where he and Claire had been sitting while speaking to Colonel

Summers on the telephone. As they looked over the fax together, neither of them spoke a word. The report was more than they had expected, and it might have been the opportunity that they needed to generate enough doubt to get the federal government to withdraw their earlier statement that the crash was accidental in nature. Sitting in the ornamental iron chair and sipping on a glass of white wine, Claire began to read the report.

"Marshall Jonah Allgood, born September 12, 1978 as Leroy Lester Jones, in Albany, New York, to Leslie and Carmine Jones. Leslie, an elementary schoolteacher and piano instructor, and Carmine Jones, a U.S. Postal worker, had two children—Leroy and his sister, Carmina, age 6 at the time of Leroy's birth. Carmina was an outstanding student, achieving the principals honor roll every year, and eventually graduating Suma Cum Laude from the University of New York in 1996. Leroy, on the other hand, was a poor student throughout high school, and he entered junior college in 1997, where he managed to flunk out in only one semester. He bummed around upper New York State for a couple of years, landing in jail on numerous occasions for minor drug offenses and petty theft charges. At age 22, in the fall of 2001, Leroy was recognized as a hero for helping save people from the September 11th attack by the Jihadists. He was allowed to enlist in the U.S. Air Force with a waver for educational qualifications. His misdemeanors were cleared from his juvenile records once he entered the U.S.A F., and he was admitted into the security service branch as a clerk."

"This guy sounds a little loose around the edges, wouldn't you agree?" Butch asked.

"There's more," Claire continued. "In December of 2005, Leroy Jones disappeared from the Luke Air Force Base in Phoenix, Arizona. No record of him was ever discovered turning up again in the U.S.A.F. personnel files. However, in 2018 a Captain Marshall Allgood was assigned to the Joint Base Charleston facility, and he has been on their roster since that time."

"How does Leroy Jones and Captain Allgood correlate in this file? Are we looking at two different people, or is that in question?"

"There is no historical records of a Captain Marshall Allgood that extend beyond June of 2018, when he was assigned to the Joint Base Charleston. His personnel record was sealed and not available for review by the S-2 Section, the Department of Defense. His presence on Flight C5-SGM12 was not coincidental. He had no flight history in his personnel folder, and there was no good reason for him to be aboard that flight, much less as the flight engineer. He was definitely a plant by someone for the specific purpose of insuring the aircraft would crash that day."

"What happened for those thirteen years when Leroy Jones disappeared until he reappeared as a captain in the same branch of the U.S. Service? And how do we know for sure that we're talking about the same person?" Butch asked. Claire continued to read the report out loud.

"Not until a request was made during the investigation of Captain Allgood was it discovered that the same fingerprints were on file for both the captain and Leroy Jones. Jones had been fingerprinted when he joined the security services branch back in 2001, and his fingerprints and the captain's fingerprints were identical. That's how we know for sure who the flight engineer really was."

Butch took a sip of his wine, seemed to stare into space for a few moments, and then asked the obvious question.

"How do we go about reconstructing the time that elapsed between 2005 and 2018, especially since Leroy Jones disappeared without a trace for those years?"

"Butch, no one disappears in our society today without leaving a trace. It's just not possible with all the electronic data available about every one of us on the planet!"

"I agree that your statement makes sense, but how do we go about reconstructing that scenario that is missing for those eight years?"

"That chore, my dear partner, is ours to figure out. If we can't determine what happened, the security of the entire county may be at risk."

Chapter 14

The Elusive Flight Engineer

"According to current research, the intelligence quotient, IQ, averages about 98 in the United States. That places us 25th in the world, compared to Asia and some European Countries. The psychologists who perform these test report that the average score is between 85 and 115. Very few individuals test below 70, as well as very few people test above 120."

"What's your point?" Butch asked.

"The odds our suspect, call him Marshall or Leroy, didn't place well above the average intellect in the U.S. In fact," Claire looked further down the fact sheet that had been faxed to them, "it appears the Leroy Jones was tested for IQ when he enlisted in the U.S.A.F. back in 2001. Would you like to guess what his score was?"

"Humor me," Butch answered.

"According to this record, he tested 93 on the standard IQ test given to all inductees when they are relegated to boot camp. That's why he was assigned to a clerk typist's position—that's about the level of complexity his IQ supported. And if that is the case, how did he manage to enter and succeed at an Officer Training Academy, and then get promoted to flying multi-million-dollar aircraft? It doesn't make sense."

"And we are sure that the fingerprints are identical for each of these men?"

"Identical!"

"If he were not the mastermind of this event, we have to ask ourselves *who else might be*?"

"Claire, let's shoot an email off to Colonel Summers and ask him to check the IAFIS database for potential matches to Leroy Jones' fingerprints on job applications, for open warrants for his arrest, and for any else we can think of." The IAFIS is a national, computerized system for storing and comparing fingerprints for terrorists and other criminals who otherwise might not be recognized by local policing authorities. The only reason a person's fingerprints would appear in the IAFIS database would be if that person has an outstanding warrant filed by any government office or police precinct. Claire went into their room, made the call to Colonel Summers, and returned to the patio.

"He said we should have results, assuming there are any, within the hour. Since we worked through lunch, why don't we walk somewhere close and get a truly Charlestonian lunch at one of the fine restaurants within walking distance of the Gaslight Inn?"

"That sounds like a good idea, Claire," Butch said. "Let's try Eli's Table, just a block down the street on Meeting Street. There's no need for a reservation for lunch." Taking her cell phone with her, Claire and Butch walked the ten-minute journey to Eli's Table, asked for a window table, and took their seats. The restaurant was quaint, as most of them were in Charleston, and the lunch menu proffered shrimp and grits, crab cakes, and other light menu offerings.

"Shall I order for you as well?" Butch asked Claire.

"Yes, but let's not overstuff ourselves. I'm thinking a salad or maybe the shrimp and grits."

"Excellent choice!" the waiter said as he strode alongside their table.

"Bring us an order of shrimp and grits, an order of local crab cakes, and two plates. Also, bring a bottle of white wine to share with the meal." The waiter bowed his head, took their order, and disappeared into the kitchen. Claire's cell phone rang, and she answered it. She took her cell phone outside on the sidewalk to listen to Colonel Summer's response to the AIFIS inquiry.

"Claire, the list of matches to the fingerprints is quite extensive, so I'm going to fax the results to you. May I use the fax number you shared with me earlier in the day?"

"Absolutely. Does the search look promising?"

"I think you and Butch will be pleased with the results of the search, and you may find it even more helpful in determining where Leroy Jones disappeared to for those eight missing years." The colonel hung up, and Claire went back inside to share the news with Butch. The food had arrived at their table, and they decided to wait until after lunch to discuss the results of the IAFIS search. They shared both dishes, ate every morsel of both shrimp and grits and crab cakes, as well as the handmade bread and butter, and sipped the last of the wine. Butch paid the check, they walked back to the Gaslight Inn, and they went directly to their rooms.

"Why don't you put on your suit, I'll go by the office and pick up the fax from the colonel's office, and we can discuss our next plan of action in the Jacuzzi," Butch suggested to Claire.

"That sounds perfect," she said, and she gave him a peck on the lips as he left their room and headed for the front desk. Allen produced the fax quickly, and Butch requested a carafe of white wine to take back to the room. Butch returned to the room in less than ten-minutes with the fax, the carafe of wine, and two stemmed glasses.

"Get your suit on, Slow-poke!" Claire said as he opened the door to the room. She had donned a tiny bikini, which looked magnificent on her firm, young body. She took the carafe of wine, the two glasses, and the fax, and headed for the Jacuzzi. Butch was dressed in his suit trunks and joined her in the 106-degree pool of water within a few minutes of her dipping her toes in the water. He slipped down under the water and encouraged Claire to join him.

"Let's read the fax first," she said. "I think we may have hit the jackpot!" As Claire read over the copy of the fax message she got very quiet. She became so quiet that Butch asked her if she were OK.

"You seem very immersed in the message of the fax. What does it say?"

"According to the official records from IAFIS, Leroy Jones/Marshall Allgood had been arrested multiple times on misdemeanor charges ranging from selling contraband drugs to smuggling weapons into military bases. He served a few years at Ft. Leavenworth, Kansas, and was released in the spring of 2018. He disappeared again for over six months, and then reappeared as Captain Marshall Allgood, assigned to the Joint Base Charleston as a qualified pilot for the C5 transport."

"Any background in his file about how that happened?"

"Nope. His file has been sealed under the National Security Act of 1947. Only those people with 'Eyes-only' clearances can view such a file."

"I think General Brown has as much security access as POTUS, so he may be able to get that record unsealed for us. I'll give him a call when we get back in the room. What else does the IAFIS report say?"

"When he was posing as Captain Allgood he was arrested in a nightclub, initially charged with espionage, then released on his own cognizance with no charges ever filed. The details and disposition of that incident is in the redacted files."

"Very interesting. First, we need to get General Browns office to get us full access to that file. Without it we will probably never have the connecting dots to place Captain Allgood in the cockpit of Flight C5-SGM12. Once we have more information about the reason Allgood was arrested for espionage, we may be able to determine who and why Allgood was permitted to retain his freedom and to remain available to possibly damage our national security. Anything else of note in the file?"

"No, that's about it. Isn't that enough?"

"Let's enjoy the Jacuzzi for a few more minutes, uninterrupted by boring facts of the investigation, then we will go back to the room and put everything together." Butch had been inching his way toward Claire, and when she put the paperwork down on the bench close to the pool, Butch grabbed her, floated her into the middle of the Jacuzzi, and dunked her under the water. Claire, not wanting to appear as the weak link in their partnership, reached under the water and pulled Butch's swim trunk completely down to his ankles. As he dove under the water to repair the damage, Claire exited the Jacuzzi with a look that told him she was a fighter and not someone to mess around with. He had no doubt about that. When Butch got to the room Claire had locked herself in the bathroom and was running the shower, washing the chlorine from the Jacuzzi off her body and out of her bikini.

"Let me in the bathroom," Butch said as he knocked on the door.

"I can't hear you. I'm in the shower," was all he heard back from Claire. She took her good time getting cleaned up, eventually opening the door and allowing a large cloud of steam to envelope the dressing area, and then she quietly slipped out of the bathroom.

"I know what you're doing," he said with a chuckle in his voice.

"Oh, yeah. And what is that?" she fired back at him.

"You're just upset that I outsmarted you and dunked you in the Jacuzzi. Admit it." She looked at him with a devilish grin.

"You know, Butch. You need to sleep eventually, and you have no idea what I might do to get even with you while you're sleeping. I could cut of some of the hair off your head, fill your Jockey shorts with you own shaving cream, or think of several things to do to get even."

"And you think you'd get away with something like that?" he asked, now seeming more concerned that he might have kicked over a hornet's nest with the dunking of his partner in the pool.

"You will find out when it happens. Until then, just be ready for an equal opportunity prank. You know I will get even. I always do!" She batted her eyes at him, smiled, and began dressing for dinner. "By the way, tell me more about SNOB."

Slightly North of Broad was a fine establishment, dating back to the late 1990s, and it was considered more of a local eatery than most of the other fine dining establishments in Charleston. Many of the local businessmen, merchants, and public figures in the city frequented SNOB for lunch and dinner. One of the reasons many of the diners explained their propensity to repeat their dining experience at SNOB was that the personnel rarely changed, the food was always the freshest in the area, and the prices never increased appreciably. That doesn't mean one could get a burger and fries for $6.00, like out on Highway 17 toward the plantations. No, the food was just as expensive as Anson's, Henry's, and 82 Queen. The charm of the restaurant was that the owner had convinced all his repeat patrons that he would never change anything that they liked on the menu, or the prices for their favorite dish or drinks. Whether or not he kept that promise is not something anyone had researched, but he had convinced enough local people that he could do pretty much what he wanted and never be criticized by his loyal customers. It took a while to earn that type of loyalty in a city such as Charleston, but Executive Chef Russ Moore had achieved it.

"SNOB is more of a local place, than it is a tourist attraction." He explained the mystique that Chef Moore had created with the hometown atmosphere concept to Claire, and she immediately became excited about their evening dinner date. "If you're going to pull some trick on me, please don't do it at SNOB. That would be unforgivable, and we would probably be banned from one of the best restaurants in Charleston for life!" Claire said nothing—just smiled that devilish grin that she could conjure up as easy as pie.

"I won't ruin our dining experience at SNOB. I promise. As far as the shave cream in your shorts—that's another question all together! What time should we leave to get to SNOB by 7:00 PM? Can we get the by foot or will we need to call a taxi or shuttle?"

"Almost nothing in the Battery area of Charleston demands transportation other than our feet. SNOB is located on East Bay Street, just a couple of blocks east from Meeting Street down Queen Street. We can walk there in a matter of minutes. If we leave by 6:45 PM we should be five minutes early for our dinner reservation." He looked at his watch, determined that they still had a couple of hours to kill before dinner, and used his sexiest voice to invite Claire to take a little nap with him before they left for SNOB.

"I've already had my bath, washed my hair, and begun to put on my face. Any shenanigans will have to wait until after dinner, and only if you're a much better-behaved host than you were in the Jacuzzi," she scolded him.

"OK, I'm sorry. I should have known better. Please forgive me for being a jerk," he pleaded. Claire looked at him and smiled.

"You're forgiven, but I'm still not getting in bed with you until *after* dinner." Butch shrugged, turned his face to the wall, and dropped off to sleep.

* * *

Butch woke up disoriented, thinking that he was in their house in Ashburn. He didn't recognize the bedroom, the dressing area, or the furniture that was definitely nicer than what they had pieced together when they were furnishing the rental unit. It finally dawned on him that he was in a nice hotel, and he immediately began to look for Claire. No one else was in the room, but Butch could smell the perfume, hair spray, and other cosmetics that she had used to get ready for whatever event which was about to unfold. He started to get out of bed and noticed that he was naked under the sheets. Although his memory was returning after his deep sleep, there were still some gaps in his memory that needed to be recalled for him to understand why he was sleeping naked with no one else in the room. He managed to get into the shower, washed his hair, dried himself, and walked back into the main room of his hotel room. The door began to open, and Butch moved back into the bathroom, peeking around the corner to evaluate whom his visitor might be.

"I know this might sound weird, but what am I doing here in this hotel? Where are we, anyway?" Claire began to laugh, although Butch didn't find her humor interesting.

"We are in Charleston, South Carolina, at the Gaslight Inn, and you and I have a dinner date at SNOB restaurant in thirty minutes. You need to get a move on!" It all came rushing back to him, and he felt better. He had thought that he had been dreaming and being disoriented had made him feel insecure. Butch didn't like feeling insecure or unsure of himself.

"I'll be ready in ten minutes," he called back to her as he plugged in the hair dryer and began to get ready for their dinner date. He was ready in nine minutes, a new record he supposed, and he walked to the patio area of the Gaslight Inn where Claire had gone to wait for him. She was reading a copy of the Charleston *Post and Courier,* seemingly totally immersed in some story toward the back of the newspaper.

"What's so interesting in the news?" he asked. "Surely you can find more interesting things to read in the *Wall Street Journal* or the *New York Times*, both available in the lobby." Without saying a word, she pushed the article that she had been reading in front of him and watched his reaction. Butch sat down without commenting on the article.

"Now tell me, do you think there's anything that interesting in the *Times* or the *Journal*?" Butch was looking at a story that he couldn't seem to take in fully. The headline on the article read as follows: *"What is a pair of detectives doing investigating a closed case at the Joint Base Charleston?"* Butch looked up at Claire with questions, not answers, plastered on his face.

"How do you think our story got out to the local press? I don't think we told Allen why we are here, did we?"

"Nope. Not a word."

"In fact, the only people who had any knowledge of our investigation was in General Brown's office, or someone privy to the conversations that went on there. Agreed?"

"There's always a possible phone tap, Claire. You know in the movies it's always a bug that gives the facts to the opposing party."

"Bugging a phone line in the Pentagon. Really? Are you sticking with that possibility?"

"You're right. That's not possible. And if our phones were bugged the Pentagon's technology would have picked up on the irregularity in the transmission. It has to be a leak from the general's office. But by whom, and for what reason?" Butch thought quietly for a moment as his mind was racing to catch up with this revelation of facts.

"Let's do a little quick inventory of our possible suspects," Claire said. "Colonel Summers? Could he be the leak?"

"Possible, but not probable. According to what he told us the first time we met him, he has served with General Brown for more than twenty years, and some of those years in a combat role. So who else could it be?"

"Let's list those we know who could have been the leak. Since it's probably not Colonel Summers, we have to imagine that it is not someone in General Brown's office because only Colonel Summers was privy to the details of our mission. That leaves Collin Blackmon, President White's administration assistant; General Leonard Lockhart, the base commander of the Joint Base Charleston, and the OAFME. I don't recall sharing much with the medical examiner about our involvement with the crash of flight C5-SGM12, do you?"

"No, and the guards at the secret facility were only peripherally involved with our access to the flight deck and the black boxes. It had to be someone who had "Eyes-only" access, and that could have only been someone at the admiral or general level in one of the major branches of the military."

"Whoa! Butch, do you realize you are suggesting that a flag officer in the U.S. Military Command is a traitor to his country, or at least complicit in that betrayal?"

"Not a pretty thought, is it?" Butch knew that they needed to speak to General Brown at their earliest convenience, and he took the liberty to call the private cell phone number that the general had supplied him for emergencies. "I'm calling the general—this may not be a good idea, but I don't think we can ignore the possibility that there's treason implicated all the way to the top."

"I agree," Claire answered. "Put him on speaker so I can hear the conversation." Butch agreed and used the speed-dial feature on the burner cell phone. The general's number was the only phone number in the address book. Butch dialed the number, and the phone rang only three times before the gruff voice of General Brown answered.

"Butch. Is that you?"

"I'm afraid so, General. I'm afraid we may have some very disturbing news that we think we should share with you before we move forward with the investigation."

"What is it?"

"It may not be what it appears, but we have detected an abnormal interest in our case from someone in General Lockhart's office. It has to be his office, unless it's your office, and I doubt that's the case."

"No one in my office knows about your mission, other than Colonel Summers and myself. I would trust my life with Summers, so it has to be coming from somewhere else. What brought this suspicion to your attention?"

"Claire was reading the local newspaper, and someone had leaked a story to the Charleston *Post and Courier* about two detectives poking around at the Joint Base Charleston. There aren't many who could have known about our mission because we have told no one why we're here."

"You're correct in assuming that such a breach of intelligence would be an act of treason, possibly punishable by life imprisonment or the death penalty. I've known General Lockhart for several years, and I've had no reason to doubt him up to this moment."

"Does he serve on any foreign relations board or commission?" Butch asked.

"I'm not sure, but I will definitely inquire. For the present time, lay low and keep your names out of the news as best you can. If you have uncovered subversion or impropriety in any form, we need to get to the bottom of it before whoever is behind it starts disavowing responsibility. Is there something you and Claire can do for a day or two until I thoroughly check this out?" Claire had been listening on the speaker phone and she had the biggest smile on her face that Butch could ever remember her displaying since they had met.

"We'll figure out something to keep us out of sight until things get sorted out. Will you call us when we are able to continue our mission. We are close to determining who Captain Marshal Allgood really was, and we think we may have a lead on how to find and catch him."

"I'll let you know when I know something. Keep this phone charged and with you at all times." The general hung up without saying goodbye. Claire looked expectantly at Butch, but she didn't speak a word. She would let him carry this part of the conversation.

"You heard the general, Claire. We need to disappear into the masses until he has a good read on General Lockhart's office. Knowing General Brown, that won't take too long, but it may give us time to be real tourists for a day or two."

"Sounds great," she winked. "Why not begin our new holiday with dinner at SNOB, on the general's tab, of course!"

Chapter 15

Rest and Recuperation

"Did I ever tell you about my R&R trip to Paris?" Butch and Claire were finishing up their delicious dinner at SNOB, happily charging the feast to General Brown's black American Express credit card. They had both decided on She-crab soup w/sherry, salmon steaks grilled over an open flame, couscous salad, and stir-fried local vegetables in extra virgin olive oil. For dessert they had Banana's Foster and had finished the meal with snifters of Grand Marnier liquor. Butch had asked Claire a question about Paris on their walk toward Battery Park, just a few blocks down East Bay Street to the end of the peninsula.

"Paris? Like in France?"

"Yep. Paris, France. Wonderful place."

"No, you didn't share that bit of information with me. Is there some specific reason you wanted to share that news now, or is this just small talk?" She smiled at him to assure him that she was not being hostile, but rather really wanted to know why he would bring up something as remote as a pleasure trip that had happened years ago when he was an active pilot in the U.S.A.F.

"The key word in my sentence was '*R&R*.' Do you know what that phrase means?" Claire thought through any memories she had of military phrases or symbolic language, but she couldn't remember what R&R designated.

"I don't have a clue."

"Rest and Recuperation is what the military deemed it. Rest and recreation, or rest and relaxation, is what the average seaman, soldier, or airman thought of it. Basically, the idea was that after five or six months of stressful combat missions, the average military man or woman needed a break for their minds to recover to normalcy. These were fully paid, week-long vacations, provided by the U.S. Government to the active-duty person in a wartime theatre. They could choose any country or major city within a reasonable distance of their duty area that was an ally, or a friendly country to the U.S.A., Britton, Korea, or Australia. I was serving in Afghanistan, so I chose Paris for my vacation."

"I'm assuming it was lovely," she said. "Did you meet any interesting and young Parisian beauties on your trip?"

"Of course," he smiled. "I was a twenty-eight-year-old hot-shot pilot, bachelor, and I had a pocket full of American dollars in my possession. I partied like it was '1999!'" Butch smiled as he remember the short, but sweet, trip away from the war and the killing and misery every day in a war zone brings. He could see that Claire was not following the logic of why he was telling this story, so he sped things up a bit.

"What I'm trying to say is that we have been given an official 'R&R' by General Brown. We have even been ordered to lay low and become part of the landscape of the locals, so to speak. Let's do as I did in Paris—take full advantage of the situation."

"I like that thought. How would we go about taking full advantage?"

"First, we plan a sunset dinner cruise, take a trip to Ft. Sumpter to see where the Civil War began, take in a play at the Historic Dock Street Theatre, have lunch at Poogan's Porch, a verified haunted house from the Civil War days, and spend an entire day shopping at the Historic Charleston City Market. I'm sure the general will have figured things out by then."

“That plan sounds divine. I’m assuming we will remain at the Gaslight Inn until all the general’s calculations are complete?”

“Absolutely. He wouldn’t want it any other way.”

“I’m not so sure about that, but I believe that forgiveness is easier to get than permission. Let’s do it!”

Butch and Claire did exactly what he had suggested. They acted like tourists, shopped at all of the historic venues, ate at the best restaurants, and took two moonlight cruises from the docks at the Battery. They made a fun-filled time of their visit to the Holy City, and when the general called them a full three days later, they were ready to jump back into the fire of the investigation.

“Butch, tell me again why Charleston is referred to as the Holy City by local residents? How does it parallel the Holy City in Rome, Italy?”

“Actually, there is no real correlation between Rome as the Holy City and Charleston as the Holy City. Let me explain. Everyone knows that Rome is referred to as the Holy City because it is the seat of the historic Holy Roman Empire, dating back to around 330 AD. Also, the Pope of the Catholic Church is headquartered there, and good Catholics believe that the Pope is the direct spiritual descendant of St. Paul the Divine, and St. Paul was the first declared Pope of Rome.”

“And Charleston? Why is it referred to as the Holy City?”

“Charleston was founded as ‘Charles Town’ in 1680, named in honor of King Charles II of England who had granted it a charter in 1683. It was originally centered more inland, but the people began to build homes on the peninsula, along with many outstanding churches with fine architectural features.

Because of its diversity of people and various church denominations, it was deemed the Holy City in part due to its tolerance of all religious beliefs."

"This is a very friendly and comfortable city. I think it makes my top-ten list of cities that I like best of all!"

"I know it's one of mine." They were walking back from a visit to Battery Park where the cannon balls were displayed in large piles, welded together to make monuments to the Battle of Charleston, when Butch's cell phone from General Brown began to ring.

"Butch?" the gruff but familiar voice came over the line.

"Yes, General."

"I think you and Claire have discovered a very dangerous leak in our national security system, but I also think the two of you can help us repair it. Are you up for a challenge?"

"That's what we've been doing since you assigned us this job, Sir. We have met challenges every time we opened a new door. So, I guess there's no reason to stop now."

"Good, good. Is Claire listening in on this call?"

"I am General."

"Here's what I want you to do next." General Brown outlined a few counterintelligence actions that he thought would help Butch and Claire determine who in General Lockhart's office had been the traitor, and what information had been transmitted to their enemies. Butch agreed, the call was ended, and Claire turned to Butch with a slight smile on her face.

"I guess our R&R is over," she said regretfully, and suggested that they head back to the Gaslight Inn to get organized. General Brown said he was faxing more information about the potential traitors in General Lockhart's office, but they couldn't speculate on those things until they saw the report. They walked briskly back to the hotel, asked Allen for the new fax, went to their room, and began to ponder their next moves.

* * *

Butch had asked a friend of his who still held the rank of captain in the U.S.A.F. Security System offices to put out an APB—all points bulletin—for Leroy Jones/aka/Captain Marshall Allgood. Butch had another idea which he thought might also yield results. They would stake out General Lockhart's personal home, follow him for a few days, and see if the heat that was now being exerted by General Brown's office would force General Lockhart or any co-conspirator to slip up or give them more to consider concerning their possible involvement with the crash of Flight C5-SGM12. It was a long shot, but they needed some physical evidence before they could blow the whistle on the commander of one of the largest military bases in the world.

"Claire, please ask Allen if he can arrange a rental car for us to use for a day or two. It needs to be more of a 'Rent-a-Wreck' than a high-quality automobile. I want us to be invisible to the general and his cronies when we are surveilling them." She agreed, headed for the lobby, and found Allen at the desk doing his routine duties as Innkeeper.

"Claire, how may I assist you?" Allen asked. She explained what needed to be done, and Allen picked up the telephone and rented them a ten-year-old minivan, complete with soccer-mom decals on the back window. When the rental car company brought the vehicle around, Claire burst out laughing.

"Isn't this what you wanted?" Allan asked, a bit confused at Claire's laughter.

"It's perfect!" she said. "I just couldn't help but laugh because Butch would not usually be seen dead in a vehicle as hideous as this one. For our purposes this will do just fine. Please add the charges to our room." Claire walked back to the room, asked Butch if he could take a break, and they walked back toward the patio to have a glass of wine and review their plan going forward. Claire had had the concierge park the minivan in front of the hotel so she could show it to Butch. She suggested that they take their glasses of wine with them and stroll down the street a block or two to stretch out their legs. What she really wanted to do was to see if Butch could spot the Rent-a-Wreck that Allen had procured for their stakeout.

"You know it's illegal to walk around the City of Charleston with an open container of wine, don't you?" He asked.

"Yeah, but who really cares in Historic Charleston? Drinking wine in Charleston is like drinking cola in most towns. By the way, she gestured back up the block toward the Gaslight Inn, can you guess which of the cars on the street is our surveillance vehicle?" Butch had not been prepared to play her little game of hide and seek with the vehicle they would be using to follow the general, but he guessed he could play along. Butch saw a Ford 150 pickup truck, a non-descript imported sedan with four doors and black tires with cheap hubcaps, a couple of Toyota or Honda sedans with little or no outstanding features, and a minivan.

"Well, one thing for certain I can tell you. It isn't the minivan! That would be too obvious."

"So guess. Which of the other vehicles would you think would be a perfect car for tailing someone, other than the minivan?" She waited for Butch to consider all the possibilities.

"The Ford 150 pickup would cause attention in a residential neighborhood, the small sedan with black tires and cheap hubcaps screams of being a decoy, but one of the two small foreign sedans would be less noticeable. I would guess either the Honda or the Toyota sedan."

"Nope."

"The Ford 150 pickup?"

"Nope."

"The ugly little sedan with the cheap tire and hub caps?"

"Nope."

"That's all of them, except the minivan." Claire said nothing. "The minivan? You rented us a minivan to spy on a top general and possibly dangerous traitor to our country? What if we need to make a swift getaway from someone firing at us? You are kidding, aren't you? The minivan?"

"Yep. You see no one, and I mean no one, is going to suspect a ten-year-old minivan is being used to surveil a top general in the U.S.A.F." Butch thought for a while and then agreed—it was genius.

"I have to tell you, Claire. That if it weren't such a genius idea to use that bucket of bolts to spy on General Lockhart, I wouldn't be seen in it for any amount of money."

"I know. Humor me. We can get up close and personal with this minivan. While I was waiting for Allen to get this vehicle rented and sent over, I looked over the fax with the additional person information about General Lockhart. He is married, has two kids in middle school, and sends them to the most expensive private school in Charleston. He belongs to the Kiawah Island Golf Resort County Club, his wife shops at the best stores on King Street, and they live in one of the historic bachelor houses in Charleston on Tradd Street. The average home on Tradd Street is over $4 million."

"Maybe he has inherited family money," Butch answered.

"Nope, not according to this workup. The FBI had ordered a background check of General Lockhart when he was promoted from colonel to brigadier general a few years ago. His background is as common as yours and mine."

"And you think he may be selling his influence, or possibly government secrets, to maintain his lifestyle?"

"Butch, you've been in the military. You were an 0-3 in rank. The base salary for an 0-3, without flight pay or hazardous duty pay, is $6,083 a month before taxes. For an 0-7, brigadier general, the base pay is just short of $10,000 per month, or $120,000 per year, and that is before taxes. General Lockhart is living at about the $30,000 per month income level. His wife plays bridge, the kids don't bring any income into the home, so where is he getting the additional $250K per year? It's pretty easy math, wouldn't you agree?"

"Maybe there's some other explanation—a rich relative who died and left him a fortune; a trust fund set up by his parents when he was just a kid; or a patent that he filed that makes him a lot of money. What are the odds that a military man who has thirty years of service in the U.S.A.F. is on the take from a foreign country? How could anyone sell out his own country?"

"It's done every day, Butch. You are just too close to the forest to see the trees. Let's create a tail on the general and see what happens. If there are no smoking guns after a while, then maybe we're on the wrong track. I don't want to think that one of the most powerful military men in the country is a traitor, but the facts are what they are. We need to know the truth and let the chips fall where they may."

"I know you're right, but I just don't want any of my heroes to be crooks, much less traitors, and anyone who gives his entire productive working life in service to this country is a hero to me." Claire agreed, and they went back to the room, dressed in average-looking street clothes, grabbed a camera, and headed back to the van. It was getting late in the day, and they thought being in the vicinity of Tradd Street near the general's home would give them an opportunity to see how General Lockhart operated off the base. They pulled onto Tradd Street from Church Street and parked on the side of the street where they could find an open area large enough for the minivan. Tradd Street was one of those streets, like Broad Street which ran parallel to Tradd, which ran the full width of the peninsula. Tradd Street was also one-way, with traffic moving from the west side of the peninsula to the east side, ending just to the north of the Carolina Yacht Club located off East Bay Street. The fax information stated that the general lived at 23 Tradd Street, and Butch was surprised that his house was one of the homes that comprised the famous Rainbow Row homes in the Battery.

"What would you like to bet that the general's home is worth several millions of dollars? Are you familiar with the Rainbow Row homes of Charleston?"

"I saw a picture of Rainbow Row in the magazine. Is this Rainbow Row?" she asked in amazement.

"Absolutely. This street, and these three or four homes that are gayly painted contrasting pastel colors, is almost as famous at the City Market or the Dock Street Theatre. Let's wait and see what happens when the general arrives." They sat there another thirty minutes until a sleek, Mercedes AMG coup pulled into the driveway at 23 Tradd Street. The distinguished looking gray-haired gentleman who stepped out of the automobile was sporting a U.S.A.F. uniform complete with a star on each shoulder epaulet, signifying that he was a brigadier general. He looked to be in his 50s, and he appeared to be in great physical condition for his age. Butch snapped a few long-range shots of the general alongside his $162K automobile, put the camera down, and observed the man as he approached the front door of his home.

"What would you estimate that automobile costs?" Claire asked.

"I don't have to estimate. I priced one when I left the service and struggled with my conscious to buy one instead of investing my separation pay in the stock market. To answer your question about cost, I imagine the new ones cost in the range of $160K to $165K with all the bells and whistles."

"Yikes! Why do men think their automobile should be an extension of their manhood? Too much testosterone for me!"

"You'd have to be a man to understand," he said and smiled at her.

"Do you think the general is our man? Do you actually think he may be a traitor?"

"That decision is above my pay grade, but I will tell you if we are using motive, means, and opportunity as the three factors that have to be present for a crime to be committed, I would say the general would be high on my list of suspects. We need to get back with General Brown and see how he wants us to handle this situation. The damage to our national security would be tremendous if General Lockhart is guilty of compromising our intelligence community for monetary gain, but there may be a silver lining for everyone if we can reach a backroom compromise with him, assuming he is complicit."

"Can we talk about that over dinner? I'm getting hungry for some Lowcountry cooking!" Claire said.

"Right after we talk to our boss," Butch said, dialing the general's cell number. He listened to three rings of the distant phone before he heard the familiar raspy voice of General Brown.

"What have you got, Butch?" The typical response to a phone call for the general was what Butch was experiencing now. He put the phone on speaker and told the general that Claire was listening in as well.

"It's not good news, Sir. I'm afraid yours and my suspicions are true. General Lockhart is living way above his means, and he's not even trying to hide or disguise his actions."

"Give me an example."

"He lives in a multi-million-dollar home in the nicest part of Charleston, drives a $160K automobile, sends his children to expensive and exclusive private schools, belongs to a fancy country club, and allows his wife to shop at the most expensive retail establishments in the city. According to his FBI background investigation file of a few years ago, he does all that on a $10,000 a month government salary? I don't think the math works for me, Sir." There was not an immediate response on the other end of the line, so Butch and Claire were silent, giving the general time to think about all the information that he had just heard.

"You're right, Butch. That doesn't look good for Leonard." Butch figured General Brown was on a first name basis with General Lockhart, and now he was dealing with the potential betrayal of a friend. "What do you recommend as your next move?"

"I think he should be arrested and confronted. I'm not sure if he will lawyer up or not, but if he doesn't ask for legal counsel, do you think some type of immunity could be arranged if he came clean with us and gave us the rest of the facts of the crash of Flight C5-SGM12? We also need to know why it was necessary to bring it down like they did, and who benefited from the crash. Should we let the MPs handle the arrest, or should we do it ourselves?" The general was quiet again, probably thinking of all of his options.

"If the MPs arrest him, he will surely lawyer up. I know I would. However, if you are able to get him into a social setting, level with him about what you know already about his situation, and then give him options to save his family the embarrassment and pain of being aligned with a traitor for a husband and father, you might get more cooperation than just having him arrested. I will have to speak to POTUS about waving charges and exonerating him from his crimes in lieu of information about the espionage, but that's going to take a day or two to put together. I tell you what I will do. Since I outrank General Lockhart, I will give him a call and ask him to meet you two for lunch to discuss some things about the crash of the C5 and tell him he would be doing me a favor to meet with you. It's almost a no-brainer for him to accept such a suggestion by his superior officer."

"That might work, Sir. Will you give us a call as soon as you know something?"

“Sure. I’ll call him now. If he agrees, where would you want to meet him for lunch?”

“Tell him to meet us at 82 Queen at 11:30 AM. We will secure a private table in the courtyard so we will not be overheard by nosy locals.”

“Stay right where you are for a few minutes and let me get this arranged for you. I’ll call you right back.” He hung up. By Butch’s watch, ten minutes later General Brown called back and told him the General Lockhart would meet them for lunch at 82 Queen at the suggested time. Butch thanked him for setting up the meeting, and the general had a suggestion for Butch and Claire when they met with the suspected traitor.

“Don’t cut him any slack. Tell him about his potential for life in prison or the death penalty if this goes to a general court martial. Relate to him that the only friends he has are you two, and for him to escape the righteous judgment he deserves he must come clean and sign a non-disclosure agreement. We will put him and his family in the WITSEC program as soon as he agrees to cooperate. It won’t be as fancy as he’s been living, but he will most likely not be prosecuted nor murdered by his partners in crime. I imagine he would be more afraid of them than us. Can you pull that off, Butch?”

“I think so, General. We will be in touch as soon as we have anything to share that’s worthy of your time.” The general hung up once more, and the climax of their investigation was just a few hours away. Now it was time to choose another great dinner venue, and Butch had a great one in mind.

“How about the most expensive restaurant in the city for a swan song?”

“Swan song? Do you really think we have our perp dead to rights?”

"I do. I think by this time tomorrow we will be flying back to Birmingham on a Gulfstream 7, eating caviar and drinking fine wine."

"What is the name of this fabulous restaurant where we will be dining this evening?"

"Circa 1886 on Wentworth Street. We'll have Allen call ahead and get us a reservation. Since this is not the weekend, we shouldn't have too much trouble getting in for an early seating."

"Every restaurant has something it does better than one of its peer restaurants, such as 82 Queen and its shrimp and grits; Anson's with its crispy flounder; Henry's with its finely prepared red meats; and Blossom's with its seafood salads. What is the specialty of the house for Circa 1886?"

"Simply, the desserts. Circa 1886 has been awarded the best restaurant for desserts in the City of Charleston. They have one dessert that has three separate preparations presented, full of chocolate, mint, slivered almonds, and fine sugar. The entrees are also very fine, focusing on local fresh fish catches and seafood from the area. Their homemade bread is the best in the city."

"How do you know so much about this restaurant, Butch? Have you been there?"

"I've stayed there a time or two over the years. It's a bit pricy, but it has one of the only five-star restaurants in the Historic District."

"You mean it's more expensive than the Gaslight Inn?" Butch chuckled. He knew Claire had stayed in hotels all over the United States when she was touring with the music ensemble after her graduation from Ashburn ten years ago, and he figured she had had to pay premium prices in New York, Chicago, Boston, and Washington, D.C.

"I'd say the price for a room is about twice as much as the Gaslight Inn. An average room rate at the Wentworth Mansion is $450 to $500 per night. Add a $250 dinner experience to a couple of nights lodging and you've spent more than $1,000—easy."

"And you want to spend $250 for dinner tonight for us at Circa 1886? Isn't that wasteful?"

"I'm not intending on spending a penny myself, but rather Uncle Sam is taking us out one more time before we leave this marvelous city. What do you say?"

"Have Allen make the reservation. I want to see a meal worth $250 and a room that cost $500. That may make the highlights reel of our trip!" Butch thought Claire was so genuine when she reacted as she had about the Wentworth Mansion, and under different circumstances he might think she would make someone a great wife. Unfortunately, not him.

They went to dinner, enjoyed the local fish, shellfish, vegetables, and the fabulous desserts. Since the hotel had an open room for the evening, Butch asked the innkeeper at the Wentworth Mansion if they might look at the suite, just in case they returned to Charleston at another time and decided to stay at the Wentworth Mansion. He was delighted to show off his pretty amazing hotel. By the time Butch and Claire had returned to the Gaslight Inn they were beat. Butch tried to get Claire into the Jacuzzi, but she said the bed was a better option. Butch had planned to suggest a lovemaking session, but they both fell asleep almost immediately when they arrived back at the hotel, and neither woke until the sunlight came streaming through the shutters the next morning.

Chapter 16

The Best of Two Choices

Butch and Claire had slept well the night before, having passed out from sheer fatigue after eating a fabulous dinner at Circa 1886 and walking home to the Gaslight Inn. They were getting ready to meet General Leonard Lockhart, the probable key to discovering why Flight C5-SGM12 was purposely crashed, and the lives of eight airmen and pilots lost forever. Butch had been reared in a typical Southern home with the fear of God, loyalty to one's homeland and flag, and knowing right from wrong being precepts that everyone in his circle of friends accepted as everyday life and moral standards. Having the option of offering a traitor to his country a "get out of jail free card" was not really his style. Personally, he thought the general, if guilty, should be hanged from the neck until dead! Butch also understood that what he personally wanted and felt was not necessarily the best outcome for his country. He and Claire had walked down to the lobby and had partaken of the breakfast bar that was ever present at the Gaslight Inn from 7:00 AM until 10:00 AM. They were formulating their conversation in advance of meeting General Lockhart, just to make sure that they didn't miss something important that needed to be said. Claire intended to record the entire luncheon with her cell phone just to have a record of what was really said, and what might be denied at a later meeting that might include lawyers for the government and the general's personal counsel.

"Are you ready to slay the bull?" Butch asked Claire.

"Slay the bull? Is that some kind of rhetorical question?"

"Well, I guess it could be considered rhetorical, assuming that General Lockhart is not whom we think he is. As an old man use to tell me as a lad, 'If there is enough smoke to fill the sky, there's a fire somewhere below it.' There's enough smoke floating above General Lockhart that his whole world could be one big fire!"

"What I think we should be careful of at this point is assuming the general is the prime suspect, when he may only be benefiting from his relationship to the actual traitor. Let's face it. The general is in his mid-50s, not one to be jumping out of an aircraft on touch-and-go landings. There are elements to this conspiracy that we just haven't discovered at this point in our investigation."

"Hence, the carrot and the stick. If the general doesn't prefer the carrot, the stick will definitely provide plenty of motivation for him to talk. We will see in an hour or so," Butch said as he noticed that his watch read 9:30 AM. "By the way, let's put our belongings together so we can make a quick exit if things go well with the general at lunch." Claire offered no major resistance to Butch's request, and she started loading all her cosmetics, folding clothes, and hanging closed into her small suitcase. At 10:15 AM Butch and Claire walked up to the lobby, greeted Allen with a friendly morning gesture, and both took cups of coffee and juice to the patio.

"Allen, we may be leaving Charleston after lunch. Please tally up our bill, charge it to the American Express card which I gave you when we checked into the hotel a few days ago, and I'll stop by for a copy of the receipt when we pick up our luggage. I will also need someone to deliver the Crown Vic that we procured from the Charleston City Motor Pool back to them after we depart for the airport. We will just call an Uber to take us back to the Joint Base Charleston where our private transportation will take us back to Birmingham. It's been a wonderful stay, and you have been the consummate host, as always!"

"We hope we made your stay as comfortable as possible," Allen said in return. "I'll have everything ready for you once you return from lunch. By the way, where are you having lunch today, and what do you plan to order?"

"We will revisit one of our favorite places—82 Queen. Claire and I intend to have a fancy seafood salad, our guest diner will probably be eating crow." Butch turned, exited the lobby, and joined Claire on the patio where she was finishing up her orange juice and coffee. Allen was puzzled at Butch's comments about his guest's probable meal, but Allen was cool enough not to ask for an explanation.

"Did you speak to Allen about our leaving town after lunch?"

"Yes. I explained it as well as I could, under the circumstances. He'll have our final bill ready when we return from lunch. He has also promised to have the Crown Vic returned to the motor pool, and he will call us an Uber to take us back to the Joint Base Charleston for our flight home. I just called General Brown's office and asked him to make sure the Gulfstream 7 will be waiting for us after lunch to fly us back to the 117th Wing Command in Birmingham. All appears to be set. Now, we just need to get the general to sing for his lunch!"

They finished their juice and coffee, tidied up the table for the next person who might use the table for breakfast, and Butch guided Claire onto Meeting Street so they could head south two blocks to Queen Street.

"I'm going to miss this town," Claire said as they walked the short distance to meet General Lockhart for lunch. "It's not a perfect place to visit, but it beats most other places by a mile!"

"Charleston has always been a favorite city of mine," Butch answered. "As the Charleston *Post and Courier* once stated, 'Charleston is where the old and the new meet in harmony!' I don't know if that is an accurate quote, but it does ring true about the Holy City. Don't you agree?"

"Absolutely. Let's see if we can put a cherry on top of that whipped cream by getting a confession from my least favorite general of all time."

Butch and Claire were a few minutes early arriving at 82 Queen, and they requested a private table in the courtyard under the glass-topped seating area. There were only four tables in that area, and Butch handed the hostess a fifty-dollar-bill and asked that she not seat anyone close to them if possible. She slipped the note in her pocket and nodded her acceptance of the favor. Within a few minutes of them being seated, the same man they had seen the evening before on Tradd Street was speaking to the hostess. She pointed to their table and the general cautiously made his way to their location. Butch stood up, motioned for the general to the table, but did not extend his hand in welcome. If the general noticed the slight lack of warmth in Butch's welcome he did not react.

The waiter came by the table and asked if anyone wanted to order a drink before lunch. Butch order a bottle of white wine for he and Claire and asked if the general would like anything stronger than wine, coffee, water, or tea.

"No, I'm fine," he said to the waiter. "I'll have a glass of wine with lunch, and a glass of water now, if you please." The general was not dressed in his typical military uniform, replete with lots of ribbons, metals, hash marks on the sleeves, and gold trim on the epaulettes on the shoulder pads. This was the first hint to Butch that the general was aware that he was in trouble, and he didn't want to be photographed being arrested or detained in full military regalia.

"What's this all about, Mr. Todd?" the general asked. His tone was anything but warm and friendly.

"We are here to offer you a couple of choices based on your actions, or failure to take action, in regard to the crash of Flight C5-SGM12, at the Joint Base Charleston last year."

"I'm not sure I know what you're referring to," he said.

"Do you really want to do this song and dance here in public?" Butch asked. "We have you dead to rights, General, and the top brass in the U.S.A.F. are well aware of your financial rewards that seem to have no substantial support, and we are here to offer you a couple of options on how this plays out. Would you like to hear what we know, and what options remain for you at this moment?" Butch had arranged with General Brown to have a pair of Marine MPs walk into 82 Queen, stand at a distance from their table, and present a sobering picture of what was going to happen if General Lockhart didn't come clean about his involvement with the crash of Flight C5-SGM12 at lunch. To add to the implied pressure of the MPs standing at attention in the restaurant, Butch and his lunch party could see an oversized military Humvee parked in the street just feet from where they sat. The scene was more than General Lockhart could bear, and he lowered his head into his hands.

"I know you won't understand what I am about to explain to you, but I had no choice but to go along with the plan to crash Flight C5-SGM12 and the coverup that followed." Butch nor Claire said a word in response. They both knew that saying anything at this point of a confession would simply let the perp off the hook and possibly invalidate the confession all together. The general, seeing that he had complete control of the dialogue, continued his confession.

"We were doing great things at Joint Base Charleston with the C5 transport operation, and we had devised a way to board or exit the airplane while touch-and-goes were being executed without damage to the aircraft and with little danger to the personnel performing the exercise. It was a breakthrough that would allow us to possibly infiltrate foreign, hostile countries without committing an open hostile act against their sovereign rights as a country. The technology was top secret in nature, and the only personnel who were aware of the ability we had achieved were those airmen assigned to Flight C5-SGM12. We told Lt. Colonel Ralph McGee, the chief pilot, that our inside man would ride in the flight engineer's seat as an observer, and that he would report back to us on the ground once the mission had been concluded. However, certain foreign powers wanted the mission to fail, and they were willing to pay millions of dollars in bribes to make sure the flight crashed and all its successful results along with it." The general took his glass of wine and drank a large swallow to calm his nerves before he continued.

"How did you get involved in the operation?" Butch asked.

"I'm getting to that part," he answered. "I understand you were a pilot in the U.S.A.F. in Afghanistan. Is that correct?"

"It is. What does my service have to do with your conspiracy?" Butch noticed how stricken the general appeared after his statement so he decided he should be quiet again and let the general tell everything he was willing to confide to them without further questioning. "Go on, Sir," Butch requested of the general, showing him a bit of respect for his rank, if not his personal actions.

"As you know, Mr. Todd, everyone in the U.S. Military takes an oath to follow the orders given to them by their superior officers. That's why I asked you if you were involved in the fighting in Afghanistan. If you were given an order to bomb a certain facility, you would do it without question, would you not?"

"Within limits, I would agree with you."

"That's exactly what happened to me. Initially, I was approached by U.S.A.F. Command to allow the observer, Captain Marshall Allgood, to act as the flight engineer on Flight C5-SGM12. No one told me at that time that sabotage was being suggested, and that I might be implicated once the facts got out about the crash. I was as surprised as you or anyone else when the flight crashed. I was contacted once again, but this time anonymously, to not look into the cause of the crash of the C5 aircraft. I was told everything would be handled and I would not be implicated in the disaster. That was over a year ago. After that, someone put a very large amount of money in my bank account, and I began to spend it. Once I had crossed that line of demarcation, there was no turning back. I knew this could only have a bad ending, but I was not willing to return to my financial status prior to the C5 crash." The general broke down and began weeping at the table. Butch motioned to the MPs to leave the restaurant and wait at the curb.

"What we have here, General, is a real mess," Butch said. "What you have done, even if your intent was not there, is commit treason against the United States of America. I think you know the penalty for such actions, so I won't waste your time or minc explaining those potential penalties to you." The general looked up and seemed to regain his composure.

"Potential penalties? Are you saying there is an alternative way for me to handle this situation?"

"As I told you when we first arrived that we had a couple of possible scenarios to offer you in regard to the action you failed to take when the crash of the flight in questioned happened. Are you ready to consider those options?" The general nodded, and Claire spoke up for the first time.

"General, we need for you to audibly answer 'yes' or 'no' to Butch's question. I am recording this conversation, and it can and will be used in a court of law or a military court-marshal if this matter become litigated. Do you understand?"

"Yes, I want to consider the options you might suggest for me."

"The first option is that we have those Marines you saw earlier arrest you, take you to the brig, charge you with violating your oath to the United States Government, the U.S. Air Force, and committing at least one act of treason. If you choose that option, there will be no protection for you, your family, your friends, or anyone closely associated with you. You will be forced to pay for your defense, and that may be difficult because all your assets, to include your home, automobiles, and all personal possessions will be seized by the government. Your bank accounts will be frozen until you can prove, beyond a reasonable doubt, that you are not guilty of treason. That, I imagine, will affect your family's ability to find lodging, the private school tuition for your children, and your membership in private clubs. In other words, you will be in jail until either convicted by a jury of your peers, and, if found guilty, you may face capital punishment for your crimes." The general was obviously shaken, not really having thought through his actions in the past, or just how much it might cost him in the future.

"And option two?" he asked in a soft voice.

"Option two could be much easier for you. If you plead guilty to espionage, give us all the information we request of you, we will request that the U.S. Marshall Service place you in their WITSEC program. You and your family will be relocated to an unknown city, you will be given new identities, and you can start rebuilding a life you can be proud of. None of your present assets will be available to you, with the exception of possible clothing and other personal items. You will no longer exist as General Leonard Lockhart, but you will be someone entirely foreign to your past. The U.S. Marshall Service will create a plausible past for you and your family, and you will be protected indefinitely as long as you keep the agreement you make with the government. You may be called to testify in court, or your testimony may be only taken in deposition, but you will no longer be associated with anyone you knew in the U.S. Air Force. Do you understand these options?"

"May I discuss these options with my family?"

"No. Did you discuss your involvement with a foreign government and possible treason against your country with them before you accepted the bribes and quietly allowed the infiltration into the cockpit of Flight C5-SGM12?"

"Of course not, but this is different."

"Really? How?"

"Because my decision affects the rest of their lives."

"And your decisions in the past hasn't affected them? Here are your options, and they are options today—not tomorrow or later in the week. Either you walk out of here in the custody of the U.S. Marshalls in the WITSEC Program, or you are arrested and taken to the brig on your own base. You choose."

"Does that seem fair to you, Mr. Todd?" the general asked as he was beginning to regain his swagger a bit.

"To be honest with you, Sir, if it were left up to me, I would pull my sidearm and put a 9mm caliber bullet in your temple. Fortunately for you, this is not my choice."

"OK, OK! I will seek the help of the U.S. Marshall Service, but I don't see them," he said as he looked around the restaurant. Butch raised his cell phone, punched a speed-dial button, and said, "It's done. Send in the Marshalls." From out of nowhere two men and a woman in suits appeared at their table. They stood the general up, and without handcuffing him walked him out of the restaurant with little distraction to the other guests. Butch looked at Claire, raised his wine glass, and toasted another completed mission.

The waiter had been waived off earlier, and Butch waved him back to the table and requested that he take their lunch order. Claire seemed amazed that Butch was going to order lunch and eat before they left the restaurant. Butch ordered shrimp and grits, and Claire ordered crab cakes with wild rice. When the waiter left, Claire could no longer restrain herself.

"Is that it? We're just going to let the U.S. Marshalls take our suspect from us, order lunch, and act as if nothing serious happened here?"

"First, we have no control of General Lockhart if he has accepted the U.S. Government's offer for the WITSEC program. We offered it—he took it. End of story. As for lunch, I am still hungry. Aren't you?" He raised his wine glass and made an "air-toast" to her. Claire responded in kind, and they enjoyed their last excellent lunch in Charleston before they checked out of the Gaslight Inn and headed back to Ashburn.

Butch and Claire checked out of the Gaslight Inn, took their Uber to the Joint Base Charleston, and caught their Gulfstream 7 jet back to the 117th Air Wing in Birmingham, located adjacent to the Birmingham-Shuttlesworth International Airport. The flight was only a couple of hours, so neither of them slept along the way. They were back in Birmingham, headed to the City of Ashburn Police Department to check in before they headed home. Butch had taken his pickup truck to the airport a few days earlier, so they drove back in time to see everyone before the shift changed at 5:00 PM. Butch was surprise when they entered the station house, and no one seemed surprised that they were home.

"We thought we would surprise you by coming home without advanced notice," Butch said to PFC Elene Connally, the officer he had left in charge and acting Chief of Police while he was away.

"No, the U.S.A.F. called us a couple of hours ago and told us they were reassigning their two airmen who had been on temporary duty while you guys were gone. They have already left to return to their base."

"Does that mean that Mayor Hannity is aware of our return?"

"Probably so, since he was the one who told us about the reassignment of the airmen. By the way, they were excellent fill-ins for you and Claire. They followed orders to the letter when asked, and they gave no backtalk, unlike some other people in this department." PFC Connally didn't look at anyone specific, but her message was loud and clear. Everyone should be so disciplined at the Ashburn Police Department.

"OK, Elene. Continue in charge until 0700 hours tomorrow morning. I will resume my duties, as will Detective Cavender. Thank you for holding down the fort. I'll stop by the mayor's office just to make it official that I am back in town and ready to go back to work." Elene acknowledged his order and returned to the paperwork on her desk. Butch felt better about being back in his hometown, in his secure job as Ashburn Police Chief, and having his pretty Chief of Detectives by his side. He had had enough of the fast life these past few weeks, and he hoped and prayed that the U.S.A.F. never came calling for his assistance again. They left the station and began to walk toward city hall. Before they could get into the building the mayor was outside giving them the 'gladhand' welcome one might give a returning hero.

"Good to have you both back in our little city, Butch. You, too, Claire. We heard so many good things about you while you were gone." That comment perked up Butch's ears. Just who had been communicating with the mayor about their performance? Butch knew it wasn't General Brown, because Tecumseh Brown just wasn't that kind of guy. It was probably someone from the general's office, since no one else knew what had been going on with their investigation. It was a mystery, but not one important enough for Butch to worry about it.

"Did you have any problems while we were gone?"

"Not too much happened, but the two U.S.A.F. security guards left in your place had an intimidating effect on the college kids and most of the residents of Ashburn as well. We're just glad to have you back. When do you plan to return to your offices and relieve PFC Connally of her duties as Acting Chief of Police?"

"About that, Mayor. I was thinking she has probably earned a little promotion. What do you think about that idea?"

"Well, she has been with the city for a few years, has kept her nose clean, and has acted very responsibly while you and Claire were on your mission. We couldn't offer her much of a raise in pay, but we can do a few things for her."

"What did you have in mind?"

"Right now she is at level two as far as income is concerned. We could probably give her an additional $200 per month pay increase, an extra week of vacation, sergeant stripes, and the ranking NCO position in your office, assuming you'll agree. You will have to deal with SGT Cumberland and SGT Green, in case they get jealous, so you need to be prepared with an answer as to why she had been elevated in rank and responsibility."

"I was thinking of making her a Command Sergeant, giving her total responsibility of the office personnel and everything that happens on the daily shifts. Both SGT Green and SGT Cumberland will report to her. If they don't like it they can either deal with it responsibly or they can look for other employment. I can't hold back one person's growth when her peers are less than capable of performing at her level."

"Good point, and I agree. When should we tell her?"

"If you don't mind, I will call her into my office tomorrow after morning roll call and handle it that way. We don't want to rub her success in anyone's face, but they will have to get on board with the promotion or get left behind."

"That sounds fine. It should be your decision how to handle the notification since it was your idea to promote her. Do you have some sergeant strips you can offer her tomorrow?"

"Yeah, that will not be a problem. Also, I think you and I should sit down one day soon and talk about the future plans for the Ashburn Police Department. Our town is growing, there are more businesses moving into the area every month, and our tax base is increasing as well. We need to rethink our equipment, staff, and other needs for the future, and present those to the council at the appropriate time. Thoughts?"

"Let's table those thoughts for now, but I will gladly discuss them with you in the coming weeks. Right now, we need to get everything ready for the return of the students at Ashburn University. We are not that far away from the upcoming term."

"Thanks for listening to me, and thanks for allowing me to promote PFC Connally to sergeant. She deserves it, and I think she will respond by performing even better than she has already, if that's possible."

"Think nothing of it. I will speak to you tomorrow when you're back in your office in your official capacity as Chief of Police." The mayor turned back toward city hall and walked away. Claire had been standing alongside Butch the entire time but had not spoken a word about his suggestion for PFC Connally's promotion.

"You have been very quiet since we arrived back in Ashburn. What is your opinion of making PFC Connally a sergeant and giving her full authority over the day-to-day operations of the office and patrols?"

"She's definitely capable, and she has earned the consideration. As far as how the other sergeants will react to you elevating her above them, that's their problem. Just from my observations since I've been working with you as Chief of Detectives, she has outworked both of those guys combined. Of course, I'm a woman and probably biased—just a little."

"Just a little?" He smiled warmly at her and they began their trek back to the Ashburn Police Department. "That's OK, Claire. If I had not wanted your honest opinion I would have not asked you for it." She returned his smile.

They arrived back at the station, informed Elene Connally that they would return tomorrow morning and assume their duties as before. Butch also told her that he wanted to speak to her in private after morning roll call, but that he had good news for her, so she need not worry about the called meeting. They told everyone goodbye for the day, and they got into the pickup truck and headed back to their rented residence.

"Claire, how would you like to go to dinner tonight at The Club in Homewood?"

"Will it involve spending the night at the Tutwiler Hotel?"

"It very well could," Butch replied and headed his truck home.

Epilogue

Butch and Claire spent a wonderful night dining at The Club the evening that they had returned from Charleston. The food wasn't Lowcountry, but it was delicious, and the wine was superb. They speculated as to the outcome of the investigation into Flight C5-SGM12, and the final destination of General Leonard Lockhart and his family since they had entered WITSEC a few days after they had left Charleston.

Without warning, Butch received a dispatch from General Tecumseh Brown's office at the Pentagon, outlining the steps that had been taken since the crash of Flight C5-SGM12 to beef up security. He also implied that the leak that had been uncovered by Butch and Claire had been effectively sealed. He was confident that the security of the nation was once more intact, and that the safeguards that had been put in place would protect against such dangerous infiltration of potential spies in the future. Butch showed the dispatch to Claire and they discussed it in at a lengthy meal that evening. They both decided that there has not been a law created that can prevent someone from betraying one's country and going over to the dark side. However, it was a good feeling to know that one's efforts may have shed new light about potential problems that might one day sink the nation. Just as Butch believed when he was on active duty in the U.S. Air Force, you may hope for the best, but you must plan for the worst. It wasn't a cheerful thought at times, but it was reality.

Butch and Claire decided that they owed themselves a little R&R for their duty to their country in finding and disabling a spy and traitor to the nation. They both put in for vacation and the planned a trip to the Gulf Coast before it got too cold to enjoy the sea breezes and the warmth of the Gulf waters. They wanted to get away to a quiet place with no crimes that they would be required to investigate, and Gulf Shores seemed like a perfect spot for the adventure.

The trip was planned, the drive was pleasant, but their peace was disturbed by the death of a fellow police officer in the City of Butler, Alabama. Butch had known the officer when they both served in Afghanistan, and he couldn't tell the county commissioner of Butler no when it came to helping them investigate the brutal murder of his friend. Butch and Claire would be immersed in a lot more than the simple death of a fellow police officer. Their investigation would cause an earthquake of findings of cult activity before the murder of Butch's friend was solved.

www.ingramcontent.com/pod-product-compliance
Lightning Source LLC
LaVergne TN
LVHW041204150826
845673LV00001B/283